D0862685

# Violet Rose

## The Encroaching Sea

## Elizabeth Cooke

*Elizabeth Cooke*

abbott press

Abbott Press books may be ordered through booksellers or by contacting:

Abbott Press
1663 Liberty Drive
Bloomington, IN 47403
www.abbottpress.com
Phone: 1 (866) 697-5310

ISBN: 978-1-4582-2101-8 (sc)
ISBN: 978-1-4582-2103-2 (hc)
ISBN: 978-1-4582-2102-5 (e)

Library of Congress Control Number: 2017906504

Print information available on the last page.

Abbott Press rev. date: 05/01/2017

## List of Books by Elizabeth Cooke

Life Savors - A Memoir
Eye of the Beholder
A shadow Romance
There's a Small Hotel, (Winner Paris Book
Festival 2015 for General Fiction)
Secrets of a Small Hotel
The Hotel Next Door
A Tale of Two Hotels
Rendezvous at a Small Hotel
Intrigue at a Small Hotel, (Winner Grand
Prize at Paris Book Festival 2016)
The Hotel Marcel Dining Club - By Invitation Only
How to Game People Without Even Trying – A Daughter's Legacy
Still Life - A Love Story

# Prologue
# THE ENCROACHING SEA

The ocean is lethal. It is uncontrollable, unpredictable in its churning. Warmer global temperatures swell the seas, as glaciers around the world lose the ice caps and melt. Grain by grain of sand is eroded from the beaches as if eaten by acid. A surge can begin ahead of a hit on shore, sucking up water, creating an impenetrable wall.

Lightening streaks the sky as that wall creates violent winds. The Bays roil like hot soup. The Sound looks about to boil over. The storm's monstrous arm encircles Long Island and smashes into the City of New York with 20-foot waves, the water rushing inland a good 50 miles.

Subways are flooded. Electric power is cut. The wind calls to people as if it wants them, and a wild fog encompasses all. Seawater gurgles audibly through manhole covers. Water drowns docks and slides over sea walls, and any grassland, park, or back yard is like a sponge.

Those who survive, those who experience the might of the tempest, are like the fiddler crabs, dug into small holes, their lives filled with turmoil and danger that can sweep them away by the wild waves. But it's not only the sea that encroaches.

People do too.

# Chapter One
# THE DEEP

**1968**

The house was bouncing on the water like a child's toy in a bathtub. But this was no porcelain tub with warm tap water: it was the Atlantic Ocean and it was cold, being September and hurricane season.

From the deck of a small stilt house planted in the sand, on Dune Road, Westhampton Beach, on New York's Long Island, Violet could see, through the early evening clouds and waves the color of steel, the top floor of a gray shingled home from the bay side that had been dislodged by the churning water. It was drifting, shifting up and down, headed out to sea.

Violet could hear people screaming. There was a woman's high-pitched voice calling 'Mercy, Lord. Mercy', then, a man shouting at the top of his lungs, 'Christ! What the hell! Jesus, help us. Where the hell are you God? There is no God!' Violet heard the sound of coughing, and strangled weeping, and finally silence, until there was the baby's cry.

It was then she ran off the deck, out of the rain, hair wet, and her pajamas clinging to her six-year old body. Violet crept under the lower rung of her bunk bed and trembled, hugging herself, until dawn. She clamped her hands over her ears to protect against the sound of the crashing waves and howling wind, but truly to deafen the desperate, disappeared voices she had heard, and the distinct sound of the baby's wail.

That wail would haunt her forever, for her whole life long. There

1

would be no escape, no way to tamp the sound or to cover the ears when the cry beckoned. There would be no possible route to avoid the inevitable.

Surrounding the body of Long Island, lapping against the piers and jetties of New York City, the ocean reigns. It colors the life that bubbles within its perimeters, on the land, on city streets, in small resort villages and farmlands. The seawater seeps from underneath, into the earth of vineyards. Its presence demands ferries and bridges in order to move people and goods across space. The tides and waves give those on land a rhythm that does not exist in an ocean-less world, a desert world.

With all its bounty, the ocean can kill. It is all-powerful in its fury. It can sweep away the structures man has created; large buildings, small enclaves, businesses, vehicles, huge factories, mansions and hovels…and of course, people.

Violet would never trust the ocean, and with good reason, ever since she had seen the sea rise up. From the deck of her father's stilt house, on Dune Road, Westhampton Beach, Violet had seen the large, two-story house, in- tact, sail by on the water. It had come from behind, from the bay side of Dune Road. The strong building was rising and crashing as it sped out into the Atlantic, and as it disappeared from view, Violet had crept under her bunk bed, as her father's house shook.

When the wind died down and the waves receded, she slowly emerged from her hiding place. Her parents were calling for her. They had not been able to find her during the earlier tempest and were frantic with worry that somehow, she had been swept out to sea. 'At six years old…she's so light… weighs nothing'…her mother wept. At last, near 11 o'clock in the morning, with a pale sun constant in the sky, she clasped her child to her.

'Thank God for stilts,' her father exclaimed proudly. 'Thank God for stilts.'

The Annas family, George, and his wife, Anastasia, with Sasha, Violet's 15 year-old brother, and little Violet, stood on the deck of their house facing the ocean, looking down at sand and water swirling at the foot of the silts. Sasha was elated. He was the only one of the family who had been thoroughly exhilarated by the terrible storm, oblivious to the danger, relishing the wind and sea at its height.

"Did you hear those people screaming?" Sasha exclaimed, his eyes lighting up.

Violet looked at him with horror. "You're freaky, Sasha," she whispered.

"No, but did you ever…?"

"Stop it, Sasha," his mother, Anastasia, cried out. "It's unnatural."

Where the wooden deck and steps to the beach had been, there was only broken lumber stretching away down the flattened dunes. The four Annas family members glanced at the landscape before them. Next door, there had been an expensive, single story home, all white, with, George Annas understood, some very pricey art objects and paintings inside. It belonged to an odd, ethereal young woman, who in summer, paraded on her deck at night in a flowing caftan, drink in hand.

Of course, at this September moment, she was probably in the city. She certainly was not there on Dune Road.

Neither was her house.

Completely gone! The only sign on the now lowered, windswept dunes, that there had ever been a house, was a garish, white toilet, alone, looking disgruntled, as it lay embedded in sand, deposited there by the arbitrary ocean.

Violet had a fearful respect for the ocean and its lethal power. As she grew, however, she learned to enjoy its charms: the summer day on the beach, swimming out a bit too far against the current, testing. She marveled at how gray and unruffled the water turned in a rain shower.

But always, always, at the back of her mind, she saw the sea rising and heard those voices calling from the doomed house.

And the child's cry.

# Chapter Two

## A RESORT TOWN - 1950s

Westhampton Beach on the East End of Long Island was a relatively sleepy town on the Atlantic Ocean in the 1950s. Coming from New York City, there was highway only half way out toward the East End, after which a two lane road took one the rest of the way to Westhampton Beach, the first of the 'Hamptons.'

"And the least expensive," was the general assessment.

"You mean the cheapest," was the more cynical appraisal expressed by George Annas. George was very possessive of his hometown. In fact, he was regarded, by the local residents, as something of a sage historian with unquestioned loyalty to Westhampton Beach.

There, the Main Street, had a large grocery store on one side named Wexelbaum's, where locals bought their comestibles and prime meats from an affable butcher named Al – who would cut to order.

"Hey, Al. Any steaks?" George Annas would ask.

"Prime, as always, George" was Al's ringing reply.

Of course in summer, the visiting population found supplies of food there too, including fresh vegetables and fruits from local farms.

Across the street was Gloria's. One went up a set of stairs to a general store where newspapers, souvenirs, small toys, beach items, candles, notepaper and cards, were available. Gloria, a plump, middle-aged woman in a challis dress, presided on a daily basis.

"You wouldn't have a needle and thread, by any chance, would you?"

this asked anxiously, by a young woman in a sundress, of the proprietor, the intrepid Gloria.

"As a matter of fact, she does," interjected Gerge Annas, who happened to be buying his morning paper at the moment. "It's not an unusual request. In fact, Gloria has almost everything," this said with a smile and a bow of his head.

As one continued down Main Street, at the western end was the movie theater, with The Patio restaurant, (which had rooms to rent above) a distance away. Continuing on, one was met at the far end of the town by the Westhampton Country Club. It faced the whole township, straddling the landscape. Behind it was an exclusive golf course for the elite club members.

The young man named George Annas, upon separating out of the army after World War II, had returned to his hometown of Westhampton Beach in the late 40s. Although he had no College education, (only Westhampton Beach High School) he had learned a thing or two in mechanical maintenance during his stint in the army – tanks, armored cars, and large guns. In fact, he was a crack mechanic, a skill that came in handy in a peaceful environment.

George got a job at the local Ford dealership on Montauk Highway repairing used cars for future purchase. Within a short time, he became a pretty good salesman.

"Hey, George. Can't you sweeten this deal for me?"

"Only up to a point, Charlie…maybe half a percentage," said with a smile and usually, the purchase was made.

George Annas was a straight arrow and a fair man. How he loved Westhampton Beach. He loved the dunes. He had grown up on them. He swam the sea – out deep and far, dove into the depths. He played volleyball on the warm sand.

In 1950, George had seen a young woman going into the entrance of The Patio at about 11:00 o'clock one July morning. He was struck by her blondness and her Slavic face with its high cheekbones and slanted eyes.

He was more than struck. He was determined, and he followed her into the restaurant, curious as to why she would go there before the lunch hour.

"Yes?" she turned to him as he entered the dim, empty bar area. "Can I help you?" this spoken with a soft accent.

"Sure," George replied, uncomfortable. He did not know what to say. Finally, "I didn't know the restaurant opened so early."

She laughed. "No. No, we are not open yet. Noon we will be ready for lunch. Come back then."

"Well...er...what are you doing here?"

She looked perplexed. "I work here. I am personal greeter and assistant manager."

"And your name?"

"Anastasia Theopolis."

"Anastasia. That's beautiful."

"It's Russian. My parents were from St. Petersburg."

And so it began. George pursued the young beauty, often taking her to the movie theater where they would sit in the balcony and neck. He even asked her to marry him in that balcony. The wedding took place the following spring.

"I love your new name," he told her. "Anastasia Annas. "It sounds right out of a book of poems."

They found a little house on Dune Road. It was on stilts, had a deck and steps going down to the sand and sea before it. In 1953, a son was born, Sasha, a devilish little boy. Two years later, they got a baby sitter (Anastasia's mother) and saw "Love is a Many Splendored Thing" with William Holden and Jennifer Jones at the movie theater, and they fell in love all over again.

George was proud working at the Ford lot. He adored his young wife, and now a son. But most of all, he loved living by the sea.

The bay separated the town itself from Dune Road on the sandy beach that was the main attraction and drawing card. The vacationers were there for the ocean itself, to bask in its magnificence, as well as the sun. They wanted to breathe in the power of the sea.

George was envied for his small stilt house on the dunes, in spite of the way it looked. He had what the visitor could not – the ocean, the sandy beach. He had it for the whole year long, year after year, with the sun and starlit nights and the wild, wild waves.

# Chapter Three

# A LAID-BACK SUMMER WORLD

Off Main, street, on a side street heading toward the bay was the town hardware store.

"Got new Deere lawnmowers just in," Davy, the owner would tout his customers. "I can give you a good price." As his was the only hardware game in town, Davy did very well for himself financially. He was also elected a Town Councilman.

However, it was the ocean side of Dune Road that brought the countless summer visitors and sun-seekers in droves. There were renters of group houses and established beach-house owners, and the occasional persons who used the beach as sleeping quarters. These were hustled off the sand by the local police (in the morning).

The population of the town of Westhampton Beach more than doubled every summer season – from Memorial Day to Labor Day – and although the locals appreciated the influx of money into the community, they really resented the intrusion and couldn't wait for fall to come.

In fact, the animosity between local and visitor, although coated with smiles, was palpable. Yet, Westhampton Beach was proud to have, in summer, such luminaries from the world of television as Dave Garroway who had a two-story house on the dunes. He sold it in 1956, for $40,000, but just before the new buyer took possession, a violent storm took the house out to sea. Fortunately, no one was home.

The house was no longer there! So Dave Garroway had to return the money to the buyer.

Some of the locals chuckled. "That will teach him respect for our ocean!"

Others, like George Annas, commiserated with Dave Garroway. "Poor Dave. Losing all that money…as well as the house!" Of course, George felt lucky – and smart – that his own house was built on stilts. "Won't happen to me," he thought. "Water passes right under."

"Garroway's rich enough," still other locals would exclaim. "New York TV fella. He's got it made," said jealously, dismissively.

TV producer, Charlie Andrews and his wife, Jean, also summer residents, were genuinely concerned about their friend and invited Dave to a candlelit lobster dinner at the Lobster House on Dune Road. The restaurant was set high enough to overlook the ocean coiling on the sand under moon and stars. It was a romantic place, and the food from the sea was succulent.

The locals were justly proud to have the TV producer Charlie Andrews in their summer midst. Andrews' claim to fame was his airing on TV of the first African-American star to have his own show. It was Nat King Cole. The year was 1956, and truly, Charlie Andrews' efforts provided a breakthrough in a very 'restricted' media, as television was in the 1950s, (as was The Westhampton Country Club).

Charlie and wife, Jean, threw charming little dinners – barbequed ribs and martinis, on the back deck of their little summer house, nestled in the bulrushes on the bay side of Dune Road. There were always elegant jazz renditions playing. The bay before them beckoned to all manner of water athletes in motorboats, on water skis, or aquaplaning, showing off in bikinis to please the captive audience on the deck. Of course, everyone smoked cigarettes like chimneys. It was a delightfully relaxed way to spend a summer evening.

Another summer regular was Charles Addams, the famous New Yorker cartoonist and creator of The Addams Family. He had a tiny house, also in the reeds on the bay side of Dune Road. One August in the late 50s, he had a romance with Joan Fontaine, the movie actress, who moved into the minute space with him for several weeks.

This brought much comment from the locals.

"Wow! Have you seen her?" was the usual comment.

"She sure ain't as young as she used to be."

"Well, who is dummy? She's still a looker," this from George Annas.

"I guess," said with a snicker.

George no celebrity he, but a true local, continued working yearly at the Ford dealership on Montauk Highway, summer, fall, winter and spring. His stilt-house was across and west of Charles Addams' and almost directly next to The Swordfish Club. The Club was, for a membership fee, a beach haven with cabanas on the sand, an Olympic-size swimming pool with swimming instructor for small children, and a decent lunch available with crisp French fries and cold sodas.

However, the Annas house really was something of an eyesore – or so some of the Dune Road residents complained –because of the stilts. It was not nearly so grand as some of the other houses bordering the sea, although these were nothing compared to the mansions that would rise on Dune Road in later years. But George's house sat up there, high on sticks, and looked silly to his neighbors.

"Brings down property values" was the general criticism.

But the complaints did not bother George, nor his wife Anastasia.

"Stilts let the wild water through," George retaliated.

But the hostile remarks about the look of the house – how 'ugly' it was - did bother the boy, Sasha. They bothered him a lot.

Of course, in the '50s, Violet was not yet born. She didn't come along until 1962. Her father, George Annas was 45 when the baby was born, and he was enchanted with his new little daughter.

Sasha was a plumpish boy of nine years old, when his little sister appeared. He stuffed himself with chips and candy bars. He also bit his nails, and acne was claiming a place on his face. Hostility toward the baby, named Violet, started from the moment of her birth. Having been the center of his parents' world for all his years, accepting this new star in his firmament was altogether impossible. He just could not and would not acknowledge she was real. He would stare at her in her crib with clenched hands. It was hard for him to accept the fact that this little creature had stolen his father's heart.

"I'll take care of you. Just wait and see," he would hiss. When his mother appeared, Sasha would be all smiles.

"She's beautiful, isn't she?" Anastasia would crow, picking up Violet in her arms. This act did not bother Sasha. After all, the two were female. It was when his father held the baby up in the air, his big hands circling the tiny waist, as if he was offering Violet to the sun, it was then Sasha crumpled inside, poison rose at the back of his throat, and he learned to hate. It would last a lifetime.

# Chapter Four

## BALONEY

The summer when Violet turned five, Anastasia, would take her – and older brother, Sasha, shopping for supplies at Wexelbaum's on a weekly basis. It was an adventure Violet loved, accompanying her pretty mother and her 14-year-old brother.

Violet worshipped Sasha, although she was often stunned by his temper and his occasional outbursts at her. It was usually after her father would praise her and tell her how pretty she looked, "reminds me of that little actress from years ago – what was her name? – ah, yes, Shirley Temple – with the yellow curls and blue eyes and cupid lips." As her father said this, he would always kiss her on the top of her head, and she could see Sasha's face. It would be scowling.

This late June day, in Wexelbaum's, Anastasia had collected canned baked beans, two boxes of Mac and Cheese, some Mott's apple sauce in a jar, and ordered from Al, the butcher in his long white apron, a dozen chicken legs she planned to marinate and cook on the grill out on the back deck.

"And you little Missy? Would you like a fat turkey," he said to Violet, with a big smile.

"No thank you," she replied, bowing her head. This was a ritual they played – Al and Violet – every week.

"How about a T-bone steak – big and juicy?"

"No thank you," again was her reply.

"Well, how about this?" and Al, broke a wooden skewer in half, took

13

a slice of baloney, folded it, and speared it onto the stick. "How about a baloney pop, Missy?"

"Oh thank you, Mr. butcher. I love that." And Violet grabbed the half-skewer topped with pink baloney he handed over to her.

The three stepped outside into the hot sunlight on Main Street, Sasha carrying the brown paper bags, Violet nibbling at her baloney slice, going round and round its delicious edges. Sasha had a huge frown and kept bumping her with one of the heavy grocery bags. Finally, with a sudden push on her right arm, the baloney pop fell to the ground in a mass of dog-do off the curb in the street.

"Oh," Violet cried. "I had barely started," and tears filled her eyes. "My baloney pop!" Then turning to Sasha, she exclaimed, "You did that on purpose, Sasha," and the tears really started to fall.

"Now why would I do that," he replied, his tone nasty.

"You did. You did." Violet was bawling.

"Cry baby! Cry baby!" Sasha exclaimed.

This remark caused Violet to cry even harder.

"Just stop it, you two," their mother interjected. "Come on. It's hot here in the sun, and Violet, you know next week, Al will make you another."

"But Sasha's mean, Mama. He's mean."

"Now, now," Anastasia said. "Let's get these things home. Do you want to go take a swim?"

And with the thought of the cool ocean, Violet perked up, but even as they approached the family car in the parking lot behind Wexelbaum's, to drive back to their home on the beach, Violet could hear her brother whispering, "Cry baby. Cry baby."

Cry baby! Like the child in the doomed house! She could not help but think it. Sasha knew how much this nickname, which he often used to taunt her, upset her. 'That's why he does it,' she said to herself. She would not forget that Sasha was the master spoiler.

14

# Chapter Five

# EARLY YEARS

Pretty in pink! That she was, Violet Annas, so pretty in pink – or lilac – or pale blue, the soft colors enhancing the prettiness of the face and body belonging to her. She wore these colors a lot. As she grew, the effect was ravishing, but in truth, the image was deceptive.

For Violet was not just an appealing little bauble of a girl. She was smart. She was curious. Her taste in books and history, as borne out by high scholastic grades, indicated an intelligence far greater than one might expect from a young girl so pretty in pink.

Violet was tough, too. She had to be. After all, her brother, Sasha, tried to sabotage her at every turn. He complained about her to his father, in particular, whose approval he so desperately sought. George Annas dismissed these carping remarks, saying to his son, "What's the matter with you, boy? She getting too pretty for you?" much to Sasha's chagrin because it was true.

Sasha had a reputation as a bully with smaller kids at school. The girls he ignored. In fact he despised them. One afternoon, when he was a high school Junior, Sasha was caught by the soccer coach, pushing a 13-year-old boy down the stairs to the locker room.

"C'mon, slowpoke. Move a little faster, ya dummy."

The coach, at the bottom of the steps, heard this, saw the shove, and not only reprimanded Sasha loudly, humiliating him before his peers, but banned him from soccer practice for a week.

After this incident, Sasha learned to disguise his animus, becoming

15

quite clever and slick at it. Suddenly, he was 'Mr. Nice Guy,' except at home, of course with Violet as his vulnerable prey.

Later that same year, there was a huge drama within the Annas family: the absence of almost $200 in small bills, taken from Anastasia's envelope for household expenses, hidden in her underwear drawer. The discovery of this theft brought the four family members together at the breakfast table, where Anastasia confronted her husband and two youngsters.

"I want the truth," Anastasia said quietly, her voice level.

"I heard Violet yapping about a rose-colored dress she saw at Stella's shop on Main Street," Sasha volunteered. "Boy, she wanted that dress. She'd do anything for that dress. She said she could see herself in that dress!"

"Sasha, "She's only a little girl," Anastasia exclaimed.

"Oh, I know, but maybe...I don't know. It cost a lot..." Sasha left the thought hanging, a smirk on his face.

It was true Violet wanted the rose-colored dress, but nothing in this world could make Violet steal! And from her mother? The whole incident was left unresolved, but, to Violet, Anastasia seemed to look at her daughter with different eyes.

One day, about two weeks later, in early fall, George noticed Sasha was using a new camera, taking pictures of the ocean from the back deck, even a couple of photos of girls in bikinis taking their last bask in the sun.

"Where'd that come from?" he asked his son.

"Oh this?" He paused. "Why, I found it," Sasha replied, head down, hands busy with the camera case.

"You found it? Look at me, Sasha. May I ask where you found it?"

"Near the back of Magic's Pub. In the parking lot."

"And just what were you doing at the back of Magic's Pub in the parking lot?"

Sasha had no answer. He slowly passed the camera and its case over to his father who took the objects.

"Oh Sasha. This is bad. Just who does this belong to?"

Sasha shook his head. "I just found it. It was lying on the ground."

"On the ground? My God! You just found it? I don't believe you. I'm taking this – Christ, it looks expensive – I'm taking it into the police station. Maybe somebody is looking for it."

"Ah, Dad, don't do that. There's nobody…" The boy was fumbling.

"You mean you stole it?"

"No. No. I…I bought it."

"With your mother's money, right?"

Sasha stood there silent.

"God! Stealing! Lying!" George Annas was furious. "I tell you, young man. You're grounded for the week – including Saturday and Sunday."

"Ah, Dad. Don't…don't…please!" Sasha declared in a loud tone. "There's a soccer game Sat…"

"I don't care. Too bad, fella. You're not going anywhere. No Saturday game. No Sunday movie. No nothing. You are going to be right here. I mean it Sasha. You're grounded! That's final," at which Sasha fled the deck with stinging eyes. He had been caught out cold!

Sasha was wild with resentment – not of George Annas, but of Violet. Somehow it was all her fault. An irrational jealousy filled him. She was Miss Perfect, in his father's eyes, the sister who always seemed to win and he the lying, stealing brother.

He rushed to Violet's bedroom and stood there glaring at her possessions, the jumble of young, feminine collectibles, that looked to him like devil's seed, his hands balled into fists.

Fortunately, Violet entered the room at this moment, before Sasha had the chance to break something precious. She saw in his expression an absolute desire to destroy. She stood there, silent, until he finally left, sullen and unnerved, and she was alone in her pink bedroom with white lace curtains overlooking the sea.

Early in his Senior year, when he was 17 years old, Sasha became sexually aware of a classmate, a redheaded girl named Maryanne. She had never given him the time of day. He determined to get close to her and began to transform himself. He lost weight, bought creams for his face to treat the acne, became captain of the soccer team, and with all that running, trimmed down remarkably. A spurt of late-adolescent growth brought him to over six feet tall.

Sasha's fantasy about Maryanne grew more and more heated as the year progressed. He had the image of pressing her against the wall at the back of the locker room, empty of fellow students after the four o'clock bell, and lifting her skirt, 'whether she likes it or not', he said to himself through gritted teeth.

It happened for real, one late afternoon the beginning of May, and Maryanne did like it. From then on, until the end of the semester, the encounter was repeated – often. Maryanne followed Sasha about like an eager puppy. He felt powerful. Now, turned 18 years old, Sasha was sure he was a man and knew the ways to pleasure a woman.

After graduation, Sasha found a job at the large grocery chain, King Kullen in Eastport, starting out in the fresh produce department. He moved up quickly in the store. Sasha was a hard worker. He still lived at home, in the stilt house on Dune Road, ('cheaper, that way' he insisted to skeptical young friends who thought he should be out on his own – for 'girl' purposes, if nothing else). "I'm saving my money," he would declare.

He never did bother with Maryanne again, much to her dismay, but then, that was par for the course in Sasha's world.

# Chapter Six

# WESTHAMPTON BEACH — 1982

The town was different from the good old days of the 1950s and 60s, after the end of World War II, and before the influx of really big money. The Long Island Expressway now came all the way out — as far as Southampton, no two-lane road as of old. It made for a swifter trip from a sweltering city.

If one was aiming for Dune Road itself and a summer beach house, one noticed the temperature of the air dropped by at least 10 degrees as one crossed over the bay to the edge of the ocean.

"Yay! Cooler at last," one could hear frequently, yelped from a passing convertible as it crossed over the bay drawbridge and reached Dune Road.

Oh, many of the Westhampton Beach landmarks from the old days remained, like The Patio restaurant (but now no rooms above for rent). It was strictly a costly restaurant. Anastasia had not worked there in some years. "Reservations are a must on week-ends," the latest maître d' would declare proudly.

The Westhampton Country Club with golf course still presided at Main Street's end, expanded now with tennis courts.

At the opposite end of the main drag, the family-owned Sexton's Department Store, a four story old building that had been there for years had long been sold.

"Hey, you could get everything there, from lace curtains to outdoor furniture — and everything in between," George Annas would remark to the tourists looking for such goods. "No more. You'll have to go to Riverhead." A number of small enterprises had replaced Sexton's: a swimsuit shop, a store selling menswear, a yoga salon, a printing establishment.

Wexelbaum's was no more – and with it, Al, the butcher – of baloney pop fame. It, too, had been replaced by a number of stores, including the exceptional, elegant food emporium, The Barefoot Contessa, with delightful French-inspired salads and terrines. Gloria's general store, across the street from it, was now The Beach Bakery, which provided pastries and cakes, breakfast rolls, and of course, fresh-brewed coffee. There were a couple of small tables with chairs inside, and a few more outside at the bottom of the steps, in a recess right on the street. Two water bowls were set out for the dogs people brought with them to sit in the sunlight and have a hot breakfast of a summer morning and watch the parade of visitors and wannabes, one of them, regularly, was George Annas.

"I have to see who's coming to my town," he would chortle to the nearest breakfaster. "It's my town, after all," and he would down his coffee happily before heading to the Ford dealership on Montauk Highway where he was now manager. Then there were the real parades – on Memorial Day and Labor Day and George would stay at The Beach Bakery and enjoy the view.

A beautiful building, The Westhampton Free Library was built off Main Street, on the street that led down to the bay, where the hardware store once stood. At the end, across the bay, one could see the cement mansions in the distance on Dune Road, facing the sea.

"Looks like a city skyline over there," was George's comment about the towering new houses that obscured the view.

On one beautiful July day, at a table outside on the street, adjacent to The Beach Bakery, Violet Annas was enjoying a chocolate éclair and an iced coffee. She had arrived earlier with her father, who had just left her to go to work. Violet was exactly 20 years old. In fact, this very day was her birthday. She had with her a book she had taken out from the library titled "The Art of Real Estate" that she was perusing, while enjoying the pastry and cold drink. She suddenly looked at her watch. It was 10:30!

"Oh my God! I'm going to be late." She headed – fast – in her new little car – a red Ford coupe- a birthday present from her parents - to Riverhead, to her Real Estate Class on Roanoke Street in that town. She was late! The class would start at 11:00 AM and it was already 12 minutes to! She was speeding on Riverhead Road when she heard the siren.

She was pulled over by a cop cruiser. The trim, young man got out of his vehicle and approached her window. Violet could see he was startled by the tiny little blonde driver in the red Ford coupe.

"You were going near 80," he managed to say.

"I know, I know. I'm late for my class."

"Yeah? You could never get there at all if you drive this fast. And how about other people? Too fast, young lady," he said, shaking his head, as he asked for her license. As he inspected the document, he noticed the date of her birth.

"Your birthday?"

She nodded. Violet was inspecting this man in his uniform. He was near six-feet tall, slender, his arms tan in the short-sleeved uniform shirt. He had dark eyes and rough brown hair and a mouth that tipped up at the corner.

For his part, the cop, name of Bud Rose, was fumbling with his ticket pad, trying to write straight. *Violet Annas. Speeding – 78 mph $50 fine.*

What he wrote down was hard to read. He handed the ticket to her, with her license.

"Here, Miss…Violet. Take this to the Sheriff's Office in Westhampton Beach. Has to be paid within 10 days."

"Oh, I'm so sorry."

"You should be, Miss…Violet. You could get hurt, driving so fast – might never see another birthday and we wouldn't want that." His voice drifted off. She certainly was pretty – blue eyes, soft yellow curls and so little, but from what he could see in the car seat, perfectly formed in her pink dress.

"I'll be more careful, officer," and she gave him a tremulous smile.

That did it for Bud. It was Violet's smile.

## Chapter Seven

# BUD ROSE

Bud Rose was 27 years old. His working life was in a cop car, cruising the area for misdemeanors – speeding, parking violations, fender-benders, summer party noise, fighting complaints, road rage – all in a days work. And then he had seen Violet, racing her red car on Riverhead Road.

When he thought of that day, when he had pulled her over, well, all he could do was shake his head and smile at the thought of her.

Bud had attended Westhampton Beach High School, then the Police Academy in Riverhead. His first job as a police officer was cruising in his cop car, working for the Traffic Violations Bureau – in other words, giving out tickets. When his encounter with the diminutive and extremely pretty Violet occurred, his chores had expanded to certain detective work when extra-ordinary events presented themselves – but his usual day consisted of his life in his cruiser.

After that first encounter, Bud couldn't help but see Violet everywhere, not only in his mind. He noticed her breakfasting on chocolate doughnuts at The Beach Bakery on many a summer's morning, as his car moved down Main Street. 'How could she stay so slim,' he thought grinning. He would sometimes get her attention with a honk and a wave and a big smile, as he passed her on his way over to Quogue on some police mission – a reported domestic disturbance or beach house break-in.

Or he would catch sight of her on Library Avenue as he drove down to the bay. She would be leaving the library, and he would marvel how, in her high-heeled sandals, she gracefully managed the steps from the big glass doors of the building, how her pink tank top and swingy white skirt moved as she walked. This vision of Violet would leave him breathless.

'Wonder what she's reading,' was only a passing thought, as he took in her youthful beauty.

He saw her at the supermarket and at the pharmacy. He saw her going into the Chinese Restaurant, Johnnie Chi's, for a late lunch, or to Magic's Pub on Main Street for a hamburger. He saw her everywhere, especially in his dreams.

Bud Rose, for the last couple of years, had been with Jillian Burns – oh not living together – but together in the carnal sense at her small apartment near The Triangle Pub, out near Eastport and the King Kullen shopping center. It was a tiny little space, but they could make out all night long.

Jillian had 'hopes' for Bud and her. Bud had no plans whatsoever for Jillian, although he enjoyed her company – in more ways than one. She was a pert brunette who worked as secretary and receptionist in the Sheriff's office. They saw each other almost every day.

Jillian was flirtatious with Bud from behind her desk. "Lookin' sharp, policeman," she would call to him, knowing he had only recently left her bed. "Feelin' strong, eh?"

Jillian was a 25 year old woman who wanted the normal things like a husband and kids, and she was willing to bide her time, as far as Bud Rose was concerned. He pleased her mightily – in fact, she was head over heels in love.

Bud was not. Oh, he enjoyed the enthusiastic sexual games Jillian provided, her long legs twining about him, but he could not shake the image of a small girl in a red car, driving fast enough to kill herself, wearing a pink dress, with bright yellow hair and a smile to enchant.

In the Sheriff's Office, Jillian continued to tease Bud with insinuating remarks and invitations, throughout the hot summer months.

"Looks like you've just had a rubdown," or "Hey, Copper. Better comb your hair. It's tousled!"

As these comments came more often, more blatantly, the more Bud winced and removed himself as quickly as he could.

Sensing his growing reluctance to play the game, Jillian became increasingly frantic and obvious, and their moments together grew less and less frequent.

"Tonight, Rose Bud?" she'd whisper coyly, the anxious question in her eyes. Bud hated the appellation 'Rose Bud'. He found it diminishing and stupid.

"Not tonight, Jillian," he would remark. "I'm really wiped out."

"I have ways to pick you up…if you get my meaning?" she would say with a giggle.

"Sure, sure. Sorry. Maybe next week." It was an excruciating rebuff for Jillian.

Bud would turn on his heel, climb thankfully into his car, and head to his one bedroom apartment near the Westhampton Beach Fire House, next to Waldbaum's Supermarket.

Once there, in the safety of his small digs, he would kick off his shoes, pour himself a stiff Scotch whiskey, flop on his bed with a sigh, his thoughts drifting to the image of a girl in a red car, wearing a pink dress, the girl named Violet.

# Chapter Eight
# THE LOVE AFFAIR

That summer of 1982, when Bud Rose had picked up Violet for speeding (and had fallen instantly in love), he had managed to watch her from a distance, wandering about the town of Westhampton Beach, but never did they meet, until one night in August.

There was a large tent-enclosed Gala in Quogue, the neighboring hamlet. The party was a charity event on behalf of East End Hospice, and the crowd was rich and spoiled. There was a band, inside the huge tent and a raised dance floor, at the rear of which was parked a bright green Ford automobile, the grand prize at the auction that would take place at 10:00 o'clock, raising money for the oh-so-worthy cause.

The Ford car came from the lot on Montauk Highway of which George Annas was now Manager. He had earned this role after years of grunt work at the Ford agency and had offered his product to the Hospice event. (He could write it off as a business expense, of course).

Daughter Violet was there for the evening, manning one of the Food Court tables that ringed the outer rim of the tent. Being a misty evening, and quite warm, the food odors comingled – making for a strange aroma that permeated the dancers.

Violet's table was elegant – with delicious items from The Barefoot Contessa. There was cold paté with cornichons and crusty bread, cheese boards with a selection from all over the world, partnered with fresh grapes, a sterno-fired brazier filled with small sausages in a hot spicy sauce. Hers was the most popular table of all, in the array of available flavorful dishes presented around the edge of the circular tent.

And there were many! There was the Italian meatball table. There was a barbeque table. There was a deli table with sliced ham and salami. There was even an Irish table of corned beef and cabbage, really very 'fragrant'.

And of course there were several bar tables, loaded with every conceivable liquor. The 'Hamptonites' did like to tipple on a summer evening.

The whole party was protected, from the valet parkers outside, to the dancing people inside, to the food purveyors, and auction tables, to the Ford car on the dance floor. The protectors were members of the Westhampton Beach Police Department, eight of them, manning the entrance gate, guarding the expensive cars on the parking lawn of the Quogue estate where the tent was located. There was even a man stationed at the far end of the tent, down near the water of the bay, which gleamed under a hazy moon.

Among them was Bud Rose. His duty was at the front gate where tickets were turned in. He arrived early, in fact just as Violet drove up, with baskets for her Food Court table.

"Can I help you, young lady? Violet, isn't it?" he volunteered.

"It is Violet," she responded with a smile.

He was able to help her unload the trunk of her car and carry the heavier items to where she was assigned.

Bud couldn't believe his good luck. Violet looked so beautiful in the palest pink chiffon dress that swirled around her little silver slippers and matched the color of her lips. She was grateful for Bud's help. She was also taken with his manliness.

Bud was near enough throughout the party, to watch Violet at her task of purveying her various delicacies to the partygoers, many of them quite tipsy as the evening progressed. She would send him one of her bewitching looks, from time to time, and Bud grew more and more entranced.

As the auction took place – around 10:30 – it started to rain, and although the tent covered the guests, the ground grew squishier around their feet, high heels sinking into the grassy surface. This did not prevent the auction from raising a sizable sum for East End Hospice, the green Ford automobile going for much over the dealer price.

"Wow!" George Annas, who was standing near the edge of the stage, was greatly pleased and highly congratulated by the tony crowd.

"Great, George," exclaimed Jordan Mather, the new owner of the green Ford, with a large house on the waterway in Quogue, as he slapped George Annas on the back. "Cost me a pretty penny – but for the East End Hospice? Fabulous cause."

At this moment, Violet had the sense to take off her shoes. The grass was wet beneath her bare feet. It felt good, cooling, because, in spite of the rain, it was a hot night in old Quogue. As the party was ending, (early, because of the weather) the crowd was pushing to get to their vehicles. Bud was busy at the front, but always with an eye on you-know-who, as she was packing up.

Soon enough, he was able to approach her table. "Let me get those for you," he said to Violet, as he took her baskets to the trunk of her car.

It was now really raining, and Violet's pink dress was clinging to her body. Her hair was flat against her cheeks, but she was laughing and the rosy lips were enough to make Bud gasp with the look of her.

Violet had grabbed her shoes, and from a side table, a half bottle of champagne as she left, and got into the driver's seat, beckoning Bud to join her.

"Come on. Get out of the rain, Mr. policeman," she called. Unable to resist, he joined her in the car.

It had started to thunder. They cowered together in the front seat, and shared the bottle between them, even though he was still on duty. Passed from lips to lips, he soon could bear no more, and kissed her passionately. She wet and limp in his arms, was lost to him. They remained in the front seat of the car for a long time.

This is when it all began.

## Chapter Nine

# TRUMPETS ON THE BAY

After the Quogue Gala for East End Hospice, after the night when Bud Rose first kissed and held Violet Annas in his arms, the two became a couple. He called her daily, at her father's house where she lived. He sent her small gifts – a pink evening pouch with sequins; a small bud vase with white lilies of the valley; even a pink ballpoint pen decorated with gold curlicues.

Violet was delighted with these protestations of love. She also relished the evenings at the movie theater where they sat in the balcony and petted, and the picnics he prepared on the sand on spectacular early September evenings – with baloney sandwiches he knew she was partial to and sweet cider.

Violet, enrolled in Real Estate School, was studying hard. She also waitressed part time at The Patio. But it was Bud who lit up her life, and although he treated her virginal self with great respect, it had become more and more difficult for them both to hold off the inevitable.

"Ah, Violet," he would whisper.

"Not yet," she would whisper back, pulling her clothes about her.

Bud would lie back against the car seat, his arm across his eyes.

"I'm sorry, Bud."

"It's okay, sweetheart. But, when? Make it soon. I can't take much more of this," at which Violet would proclaim her love for him, how soon enough they would really be together. "I'm not trying to be a tease, I swear. It's just, my father…"

"I know. I know. And the Catholic church."

"That too, Bud. That too."

Christmas approached and with it, all manner of preparations for a festive holiday. George Annas always had a lighted tree, adorned with bulbs, out on his deck (much to the consternation of disgruntled neighbors).

Violet was in turmoil over what to get Bud for a Christmas present. He was so centered on his police-life, so dedicated to his cruiser car, that it made for a problematic decision. He did dress up when they went out, so she decided on a handsome belt and matching wallet in dark brown leather. The wallet had his initials: BR in gold.

On Christmas eve, a mild evening for December in the Hamptons, Bud took Violet to a special dinner at Trumpets, the grandest restaurant in the area of Eastport, with windows overlooking Moriches Bay. The sunset reflected on the water was glorious. A silver gull perched on one of the bulkheads outside in the bay, quiet and alone. The house across the way with its gabled roof looked as if it were an Edward Hopper painting.

When they were seated by the window and viewed the purple and orange sun sinking into the sea, over a glass of Pinot Noir for each, Violet presented Bud with the belt and wallet. He was truly touched and delighted with the gifts. "Beautiful!" he exclaimed. Then, reaching into the pocket of his blazer, he pulled out a small box.

"Violet, this is just a small present – for the moment – but somehow – because you seem to be so much a part of the ocean, I couldn't resist." He handed her the box, which she opened quickly to see, nestled in black velvet, a golden starfish.

"Oh," she said. "Now THIS is beautiful…Oh, Bud, I love it."

"It's a pin," he explained – "to wear on …"

"Oh, I know what to do with it," she said with a smile, taking the shining starfish from its nest and pinning it onto the pink cashmere sweater she wore. "Oh, Bud," she gushed. "My starfish. I'll never take it off."

"Never say never," he said with a laugh. Then, soberly, "There'll be other presents. More important presents," at which she gave him that melting smile with which he was so captured.

They ordered more wine and then crab cakes with rémoulade sauce and shrimp tempura with jasmine rice and looked into each other's eyes.

"I had to bring you here," he whispered. "Trumpets has a motto. 'If you love her, bring her here,' and I did and I do and I want to marry you."

Violet dropped her fork, which she had been holding, mesmerized by his words.

"Marry me?" she whispered back. "You want to marry me?"

"Oh, I know you're young. We can wait until your ready, naturally, but I want you to be mine. I want to know if you want me to be yours – on a permanent basis, that is," he said in a voice that touched her heart.

Violet sat back. They were across from each other. The table for two was small. She reached across to the back of his neck and pulled his face to hers and kissed him full out, right there, in front of the whole restaurant. She didn't care.

Neither did he, so lost was he in her response.

When their lips separated and each belonged again to its owner, Violet whispered, "no dessert," and with that, Bud called for the check and the two swiftly left the restaurant and got into Bud's father's truck that he used for non-police purposes. In the front seat, the two were ravenous together, and Bud quickly drove back to Westhampton Beach and Dune Road, towards George Annas' house, which he drove right past and up to the Quogue Beach Club.

Bud drove the truck into the parking lot of the empty club, now closed for the winter. The two descended from the vehicle and with arms around each other, went down on the beach, no picnic this time, and lay down together on the sand, which was December-cold beneath them. The heat between them cancelled out any chill, for it was white hot.

Violet noticed the ocean was like glass, under an ice chip of a moon. The waves seemed to be awaiting – for what? And then it happened, all the longing and desire burst upon them, like a raging summer storm that rises. The sand beneath her felt so primal, she knew that the two of them – this Bud, this Violet - were part of the earth, here at the water's edge, with water at their feet.

Violet knew, too, that although the tide would wash away the indentation of their joined bodies in the sand, the sea could not erase the image of the passionate moment experienced together. Bud and Violet. Bud and Violet. It was there, written in the sand, permanent under the tidal waters, forever.

# Chapter Ten

# REAL ESTATE

Violet passed her Real Estate test. It was hard. The exam took place in Riverhead. The course had taken seven months for her to complete, but it was worth it. She quickly was offered a job at Brandeis Realty on Main Street, where there were pictures of high-priced properties in the front glass window and a desk in the center of the office where Violet first presided for her job.

Brandeis Realty was owned by a sharp, attractive woman named Bethany Brandeis. Divorced, (more than once) Bethany was in her early 40s but didn't look it. With swingy hair, and a taut body, she was bold and sassy and immensely appealing to men, flirtatious and a challenge, partly because she was so bright and partly because she oozed sex appeal.

She liked Violet, found her so lovely to look at – a great draw to new customers. And for Bethany, a beautiful girl was no threat. Never had been. Ms. Brandeis was that sure of her own appeal.

"Now Violet. All I ask is that you answer the phone with a lilt. When you say 'Good morning, Brandeis Realty' I want you to say it with a smile in your voice that they can hear through the wires," she instructed her new employee.

"I'll do it, Ms. Brandeis."

"I'm sure you will, Violet. And call me Bethany. And Violet, this is only the beginning. You will be doing all sorts of sales work – open houses – showing properties – in due course. But I do need you for the moment at the front desk."

35

Of course, Bethany had an ulterior agenda with young Violet. The focus of that agenda was Violet's father, George Annas, whose stilt house property was in the most prime location on Dune Road, perched up there at the top of a hill, facing the ocean, directly next to The Swordfish Club on one side and a new, huge cement mansion three stories tall on the other. The fact the Annas house was on stilts made it unattractive and brought rude comments from all the wealthy homeowners that ruled the beach.

Bethany had looked up the fact that Annas had bought his house in 1951 for $29,000. The new cement mansion now directly next door had cost $1,500,000 to build. The owner was a very rich carpet tycoon. He was outraged, that from his bathroom window, he had to look at George's "ridiculous' house – if you can call it a house – and they're always cooking barbeque out on the deck. Ruins the view! And the smell!"

Bethany was determined to get the listing through Violet – even though George Annas was even more determined to keep his house. He loved it. Loved the simplicity. Loved his view of the sea and had no intention of selling, no matter the price.

George Annas did not know Bethany, did not know of her skills of persuasion and manipulation. All he knew was, as of this moment, that Bethany Brandeis had his young daughter working for her in the realtor's office daily.

Bud Rose would drop by at least twice a week and take Violet out to lunch – usually across the street at Magic's Pub, where they would share a plate of French fries and split a BLT, oblivious to those around them.

On weekends, through that winter and following summer, Bud would occasionally persuade Violet to come to his apartment near the Fire House.

She would always protest a little, but in the end, they would lie together, blissful, and so in love. Violet had learned to protect herself from pregnancy, and although these sexual encounters were not often, and they were careful, the intensity of their lovemaking made her fearful of a baby every time.

"I love you Violet. I need this more often. Please don't make me wait so long."

"Oh Bud, I love you too, but I always feel we should wait."

"For what? You know I'm committed to you. Aw, why, darling? You know how much I care…how much I need you." This would convince her to embrace him again, their passion as unchecked as the ocean, Violet thought, as uncontrollable as the violent waves that beat the shore.

## Chapter Eleven

# LOSING GAME

Jillian Burns was aware of the frigid vibes she was beginning to receive from Detective Bud Rose, her once 'intended'. Although she had always realized, the 'intended' part was on her side only, yet the hope for a future for the two of them clouded any judgment over which her saner self presided.

As the winter progressed and summer days came upon them again, Jillian sensed Bud's coolness, which only whipped her into a frustrated lather. Oh, he still came to her bed – but it was rare, a perfunctory encounter at best..

"Sweet Rose Bud,' she would coo to him hopefully, not realizing how he despised this nickname. "My Rose Bud," she'd breathe as she lolled on the pillow, watching him dress hastily and beat his retreat.

These short trysts became less frequent, as Bud's self-disgust with the sneakiness of the whole business grew. He felt such guilt. If Violet ever suspected…He was terrified she might find out. It was so different being with Violet. He was emotionally hers, a feeling he had never experienced. What happened with Jillian was so mechanical and meaningless Bud wondered why he bothered with the receptionist.

"Old habit, I guess," was his rationale. "Besides, I'm not married…when Violet and I get engaged…well, then I'll quit."

So, once in a while, he still met with Jillian. He answered the call for a 'quickie' (in his mind), excusing himself before the act by convincing himself that he was a red-blooded, full-grown man with needs, going through a sexual release.

He found for himself yet another excuse. Violet did not allow him the ecstasy they shared often enough. Once they were married, now then, she would be his all the time.

Jillian had to face Bud almost daily in the office. He was polite – but– "can you spring out for lunch?" from him, or "later – around 7:00 – your pad?" said with a wink – these little invitations were few and far between. Not nearly often enough, Jillian said to herself, and wept into her pillow at night.

How could she compete with a doll-like creature like Violet Annas. Oh, she knew! Jillian had seen the couple together. How could she not – at the movie theater; Violet riding in Bud's father's truck along side her smiling off-duty cop; at Johnnie Chi's, eating ribs and egg rolls.

One snowy night in February, Jillian was there in the corner of the Chinese restaurant, with her mother and saw Bud and Violet on the far side of the room. The two lovers shared bites of shrimp dumplings and laughed into each other's eyes. Jillian watched from lowered lids. Her head drooped over the stirfry before her. She could not eat, only played with the chopsticks, until pleading a bad stomach ache, she suddenly called for the check.

"C'mon, Mom. We're leaving."

"But, Jillian. I'm not finished."

"Oh, yes you are," the daughter announced rudely, rising and pulling at her mother's arm. "C'mon. We're going."

Her mother swallowed her last bite, mumbling, "Jill, what's the matter with you," and the two left quickly.

That particular evening, after dropping her mother off at her house in East Moriches, Jillian returned to her one bedroom apartment near the King Kullen shopping mall in Eastport, more bitter than ever she had been.

Her feelings were not yet anger. They were self-pitying and acrid in her mouth, tasting like salt and tears at the back of her throat.

Violet Annas! Just what could she do to upset that pushy little apple cart? What could she do to retrieve the loving arms of Bud Rose and their acrobatics in bed – for they were very physical - in unexpected positions, inside out, upside down and side ways. Jillian was sure that little Miss Violet was no match for her in that department.

Bud had told Jillian she was, "amazing – so agile – almost double-jointed. How do you do it?" said with a laugh, and he had meant it.

Oh, those were such good times - to have Bud beside her in her bouncy bed with his lean body embracing hers.

Jillian was quite sure Violet Annas had no idea of what Bud and she were up to. It had been going on for a couple of years – now less and less, of course, because of his infatuation with what Jillian thought was a simple-minded 21-year-old blonde cupcake.

Violet had come into the Sheriff's Office on occasion to drop off a sweater of Bud's (once), or another time, a flashlight from his father's truck. She treated Jillian as if she were a piece of necessary furniture – at least Jillian took it that way – oh, polite enough, but as if the tall, brunette receptionist was just matter of fact and efficient, not the sexy little piece Jillian fancied herself.

'Huh! Well, you just wait, Missy,' Jillian exclaimed to herself. 'I'm going to make you a good friend! We're going to be big buds! I'll butter you up like no one ever has, and Bud Rose is going to have a nervous breakdown, so afraid he'll be of exposure.'

'I can tease the bejeezus out of him with the threat of blackmail, so much so that Violet Annas will be nothing but a bad, dangerous dream. He'll realize that Jillian Burns is no one to toy with! In due course, Bud will be back with me in my bed.'

# Chapter Twelve
## COUNTER SEDUCTION

Just how to approach Violet? It was problematic because Jillian and the younger girl surely did not run in the same circles. Jillian knew that Violet worked at Brandeis Realty on Main Street, not far from the Sheriff's Office. She also knew Violet's brother Sasha. He had been a year ahead of Jillian in high school, and she saw him occasionally at the King Kullen supermarket where he worked.

But how to reach out to the girl, that was the question, and how to make her trust Jillian with her secrets.

Then, it came to her. She had seen Violet frequently breakfasting at The Beach Bakery, outside in the sunlight.

The next day, after having seen Bud and Violet the night before at Johnnie Chi's, Jillian made her way up the steps to the counter within the bakery, ordered coffee and a doughnut, and proceeded to seat herself, outside next to the steps.

It was a cloudy day, but, for February, warm and pleasant enough. In a short time, she saw Violet. She was crossing Main Street toward The Brandeis Realty office. 'Damn it,' Jillian thought. 'No breakfast?' But in mid-step, Violet paused, turned and approached The Beach Bakery.

She brushed by Jillian, who looked up at her and smiled. "Oh, hi Violet," and Violet smiled back with a little nod.

She returned with a cup of hot chocolate and a fresh croissant and Jillian said sweetly, "Join me?"

"Okay," was the reply. "That's nice of you."

Because of the winter overcast, Jillian and Violet, sitting at the little table, were the only ones there on the street. They were quiet for a moment enjoying the breakfasts on which they munched, warm in sweaters and scarfs. Actually, the air was quite refreshing.

Finally, Jillian asked, "How long you been at Brandeis?"

"Since last fall," Violet responded. "And you? You're at the front desk, right, with the Sheriff's office? How long you been there?""

"Seems like forever," Jillian laughed. "No, I guess it's been three years. My God, I can't believe it. Three years."

"You like it?" Violet asked.

"It has its perks," Jillian said. "Yeah. Some real benefits." (Like sex with Bud Rose!) "And you? What's it like over there?" She tilted her head toward the realty office.

"Oh it's fine. I'm getting out more…not just being receptionist…oh, I don't mean receptionist is a bad job," she said, blushing, "it's just, well, you know, confining."

"Doesn't have to be," Jillian sniffed. At that moment, she noticed the gold starfish pin attached to Violet's cashmere sweater. "My, that's pretty," she exclaimed.

"Yes. I love it. It was a present," Violet said, patting the piece of jewelry at the throat of the turtleneck sweater.

"So, you meet people…you know… Look. You are a very pretty girl. You must meet…you know…men." Jillian's expression was opaque, curious, so much so that Violet burst out laughing. She was not sure why. It was an uncomfortable laugh.

At this very moment, they both noticed a cop cruiser on Main Street coming towards them. Of course, it was Bud Rose in the driver's seat. They both waved at the same time, smiling gaily, as Bud's jaw dropped.

"Men, oh men," Violet was saying. "No need to meet any more. I'm already taken."

"Good for you," was Jillian's remark. "But be careful, honey. 'A man is a two-faced' as they say in the song. Be careful." And with this admonition, Jillian rose. "Well, I got to get to work. Let's do this again."

"Sure," said Violet, fumbling with her purse, as she stepped away from the table. "Sure. We'll meet again."

44

As Violet walked slowly up Main Street to the realtor's, Jillian watched. Her face was a mask.

It didn't take long before Bud came into the Sheriff's Office and confronted Jillian who sat primly at her desk. He stood before her, red faced. This gave her great satisfaction. He was one nervous cop!

Finally, she ventured, "What's the matter, Bud?'

"What do you mean what's the matter? Nothing's the matter."

"Oh, good."

"What were you doing at The Beach Bakery this morning?"

"Eating breakfast. What else"

"Yeah, sure." He began to pace before her desk.

At this moment, John Schroeder, a fellow policeman, poked his head into Jillian's office. "Hey, Jill. You got the extra ticket books yet?"

"Sure, John. Right here," and she swung around to grasp a book from the top of a pile stacked on the back windowsill.

"Here you are, John," she said with a big smile.

Bud still stood there, hands twitching. He had no idea as to what Jillian might suspect about Violet and himself. He had never mentioned her name, much less his intense feelings for her. God no. Jillian would flip out, and man, she had a temper!

"Did you want something, Bud?" Jillian asked, coy and simpering. "Maybe tonight?" Her voice was insinuating, provocative.

"Can't tonight. Got an appointment." There was a pause. "That blonde girl...you know, the one you had breakfast with..."

"She and I have breakfast all the time," Jillian responded, an utter lie, but she could literally see the skin crawl at the back of Bud's neck.

"How do you know her?"

"Why, Bud?" she responded, all innocence.

"Oh, I don't know. She just...well, she just doesn't seem to be...you know... your type."

"Well, of course she's not, and she's SO much younger."

"Er…what'd you two have to talk about?" he said, moving closer to Jillian's desk.

"Oh, you know…men…stuff like that," she said with a laugh, just as her buzzer rang summoning her into the inner office. "Oops," she said. "Gotta go, Bud, but maybe tomorrow night…if you don't have another appointment," said pointedly.

Swishing past him, she gave a lewd little lick of her lips as she passed. "Tomorrow, Bud? Better be there," and before he could answer, she was gone.

Christ, he thought, sinking into the chair in front of the desk. What in hell were they discussing together, Violet, his love, and Jillian, who was suddenly his dirty little secret. She's dangerous, he thought. If Violet – little Catholic, adorable Violet, should ever get wind of the Jillian connection, he was done for. There was no one in this world he wanted more than Violet. She was the love of his life.

But what in God's name could he do to keep Jillian quiet. "Just keep on doing Jillian like I'm doing her, I guess – until it's too late and Violet and I are married. Jillian would have to respect that," he mumbled out loud to himself.

## Chapter Thirteen

# BALANCING ACT

The next weeks became an excruciating balancing act for one Bud Rose. Jillian Burns was suddenly beyond needy. She was demanding. He thought of every possible excuse: "My mom's sick," or "Gotta job over in Quogue."

Or even, "I'm tired," which brought the response from Jillian, "That's no excuse, baby. I'll expect you around 7:00…I'll make …your favorite dish…" said with an insinuating smile. He was growing more and more disgusted, but also more and more fearful of discovery.

He had to comply, at least once in a while. He had seen Violet and Jillian breakfasting several times of late. When they were not sitting outside of The Beach Bakery, as he passed by in his car on Main Street, he would stop and go in for a coffee and more than once, they were sitting together inside the sweet shop, sipping their hot beverages and munching on pastry.

He was always met with a happy hello from both and would go to his cruiser parked on the sidestreet and wait until he saw them leave. It was killing him.

What DID they talk about? Was it about him? The very thought made him pale and sweaty.

One evening, mid-March, Bud was with Violet at his apartment. It was pouring rain and cold. He had bought a pizza he would heat up in his small oven, and a couple of bottles of Pinot Noir.

Violet was sitting on the bed, feet tucked under her, as seductive a creature as ever he had seen, but there was a difference in her demeanor. He couldn't put his finger on it. Perhaps it was his own guilt speaking to him inside, but whatever the reason, he had to ask.

"Is something bothering you, Violet?" He sat down beside her on the bed.

"No, Bud. Not really."

"What does that mean?"

"Well…let me ask YOU something? How do you know Jillian?"

He stood up. "She works in the office. You know that."

"Well…you know, she's odd… I mean, I can't figure her out, why she always wants to eat breakfast with me…like we're old friends. We're not, you know. She's…"

"Maybe she's lonely," he said, his voice raspy.

"She's so darn curious too…always trying to make me talk about boyfriends…what she calls 'my love life'."

"What do you say?" Bud plopped down beside Violet again, close, protective, afraid of what might come.

"Well, I make stuff up. And I certainly don't say anything about you! It's none of her damn business. I know she works with you and the last thing for her to know is that you and I…"

"Are in love?" Bud said, his face flooded with longing and…relief. "No, no, she should never know that, darling."

"And she never will," Violet said with a little laugh.

"No, she never will," he said, knowing full well the truth would be out soon enough, as he tumbled Violet over on the bed and proceeded to prove his adoration in every possible masculine way.

They were busy together until after midnight, pizza long forgotten, and the second bottle of Pinot Noir finished and empty on the floor beside his bed.

For Bud, the balancing act continued. He was a very busy fellow, between the two women and keeping them as unaware of what was going on as possible. Violet seemed to know nothing of Jillian's place in his life, thank God, he thought. But how long can that last.

It was Jillian who was becoming more and more problematic. "She's ready to blow the whistle on me whenever it suits her. I've gotta do something. I'm exhausted with this."

Bud decided Jillian be damned. He would take matters into his own hand, speak to Violet's father, get the ring, and get married in the summer.

# Chapter Fourteen

# MOMENTS OF TRUTH

Bud Rose drove his cruiser along Dune Road, past The Swordfish Club, and turned into the driveway of George Annas' house. He knew George would be alone. Violet had told him that this particular Sunday afternoon in late April, she and her mother and brother were attending a fund raising event at the Catholic Church over on Meeting House Road in Westhampton, near the hamlet of Quiogue.

Bud got out of his cop car. He climbed the stairs to the entrance of the house, walking past the tall stilts that lifted the structure high above the dunes. He paused on the stoop and raised a hand to tap on the door, but George Annas who had been reading in the living room, was there before Bud's hand touched the wooden frame.

"Yes, Bud." George had seen him before, met him about town, the friendliest of the local policemen. He also knew that Violet was seeing Bud on movie dates and little dinners. "Is this a business call?" George said with a smile. "Am I in trouble?" again a big smile.

"No, no, of course not, Mr. Annas. I 'd just like to talk to you…it's a personal matter."

"Well, come in, please." George led the way into the small living room that faced the ocean, a large glass window embracing the view. "Can I get you something? A beer?"

"No sir. I'm in the cruiser so I better not."

"Please sit." George lit a cigarette, first offering his pack to the young officer. "What can I do you for?" he said, laughing at his little joke.

"Well…" Bud was for the moment speechless. "Well, sir…"

"Hey Bud. Call me George," the older man interjected.

"Yes, sir…George… well, it's about Violet."

"Violet? She's in trouble – not her old man?" George said facetiously.

"Oh no," Bud said, laughing, George's words breaking the ice. "You know, we have been getting close. We've been seeing each other now for over a year and well, sir…"

"George."

"Well, George, I wanted to ask you…how do they put it … for her hand…I want to marry her." Bud blurted this out.

George looked at him, stubbed out his cigarette in an ashtray. "Well, well. Violet is a special girl." The father got to his feet, paced a little before the window, his back to Bud who was on tenterhooks. "She's my little girl. I always knew there would come a day…" Then turning to Bud abruptly, he asked, "Does she love you?"

"She says she does. I surely love her and yes, she tells me she loves me. A lot."

"You know, the Annas family is Catholic. Oh, I'm not as regular as my wife and kids – but Violet is. She's a pure girl."

"I respect that, sir…George. My sister Josie is married to John Cassidy – you know he owns the liquor store over in Eastport. He's Catholic. I'll do whatever it takes – whatever Violet and you want me to do. I love your daughter…George. I love her with all my soul." Bud rose from the armchair where he had been sitting. "All I want is to make her happy."

"Well, I guess, Bud, the rest is up to her…up to Violet. If she wants you – and I can't say I blame her," George said, eyeing the young man, "it's her call. I'd be happy to have you as a son-in-law." With that pronouncement, the two men embraced.

Bud bought Violet a ring. It was a small square-cut diamond. It took him a long time to decide on this particular one that he bought at The René DuBois jewelry store next to King Kullen.

"If the ring should be the wrong size for her finger, we will be glad to size it for her at no cost," the girl behind the counter told him.

"Better not cost…" Bud mumbled. He was really blowing his budget with this purchase, but it was for Violet, and he wanted the best because she was the best thing ever in his life.

He took the ring in its black velvet box, put it safely in his pocket and tried to decide the time and place for its presentation.

It was early May, balmy in the evening. He decided the special moment must take place on the beach with the Atlantic to bless them and the sand to be their bed of love – as it had been – that first time, almost one year ago – when they both knew they would cleave together forever.

Bud told Violet he had a surprise for her. One Friday evening when the moon was full, he bought a chilled bottle of champagne, picked her up in his father's truck and headed for the Quogue Beach Club parking lot. The Club had not yet been opened for the summer. He parked, and taking his girl by one hand, the bottle with two glasses in the other, they crossed the tarmac, mounted the stairs to the small gazebo, descended the stairs on the other side, and reached the beach.

They stood there, looking up at the sky, moonstruck and in awe. The light from above drew a golden path on the water, quietly rippling before them. Violet had managed to clip her starfish pin on a ribbon in her hair and it gleamed there, sending sparks of light around her upturned face. Bud felt he had never seen anything so beautiful and he leaned to kiss her parted lips and dropped the bottle (it did not break), and they sank together at the water's edge.

On their knees they clung together, and he reached in his pocket and withdrew the velvet box.

"I want you to stand up," he said, his voice hoarse. She did.

Bud proffered the open box with the diamond ring inside and said almost inaudibly, "Will you marry me, Violet?"

There was a long pause. "Yes," she said, crying to the moon. "Oh yes, Bud. I'll be your wife. Forever."

And they fell together on the sand. Violet could feel the waves lapping at her feet, now bare, as was the rest of her, and there, naked in the moonlight, the two committed one to the other.

Only later did they get to the champagne.

## Chapter Fifteen

# THE BEST MAN

Bud decided to approach Sasha to be best man at the wedding. He chose him consciously, not that he liked him particularly or thought him a true friend. No. Not at all. His cop buddy, Mack Rhodes would have been his first choice. Bud chose Sasha because he thought that by doing so, he might ease the friction between his new little bride and her brother. He asked him for Violet's sake, although Bud did not mention this to her.

Bud always thought that Violet's references to Sasha – of certain incidents in the siblings' past – were exaggerated, although Violet never went into great detail. She indicated – with a shrug of the shoulder – the antipathy that had plagued her. She would say, "Sasha never liked me" or "I know he thought Dad preferred me" (her father did!) or "he could suddenly lose his temper…I mean, like a blast from outer space!"

Bud approached Sasha at his job at King Kullen, one early May morning. He pulled into the parking lot and went directly to the glass cage-like office where Sasha presided. He knocked on the window and Sasha saw him from behind his desk and came forward immediately.

"Hey, Bud. What's up?"

"Can I come into your office?"

"Sure. Just go around to your left. There's a door."

Bud entered at the back. Sasha sat at his desk. "Anything wrong?"

"Why does everyone think something is wrong if I want to see them?" Bud said with a little laugh.

"Because you're a cop! Why else?" Sasha said, his eyes glinting.

"Well, I'm not on cop business. I have a personal request."

"And?" Sasha said with a raised eyebrow. "That sounds even worse."

"I hope you won't think so. It's just that… well, I'll just say it. You know Violet…I'm going to ask her to marry me."

"Oh, really?"

"Yes, and I wondered if you would be my Best Man."

This brought Sasha to his feet. "IF she says yes," he said coldly. "But why would you want me?"

"You're the brother of the woman I love. There's no one in my own family – no brother or cousin. You are part of the family I am joining. It would be special if you would accept."

"In other words, I'm the last resort. Hmm. Well, I guess so, Bud, if you want me." Then with a sly look, "Does Violet know you're asking me to be your Best Man?"

"No, Sasha. Not yet. I'll tell her tonight."

Bud thought Sasha's participation in the ceremony might provoke a kind of loyalty – to the new marriage, a realization for Sasha that Violet would now be an adult, married woman and out of her brother's life.

When he discussed his choice with Violet that evening over hamburgers at The Triangle Pub she was silent.

"You really wanted Sasha?" she asked softly.

"Yes, darling. Thought it might heal old wounds."

## Chapter Sixteen

# JUDGEMENT DAY

Through the previous winter, Jillian had tried to be patient with Bud Rose.

Then came the night in mid-May. It was pouring rain. Bud had told her he was dropping by her apartment, and he arrived near 7:00 o'clock. Jillian greeted him at the door, in her terry cloth bathrobe, wet from a shower.

"No, Jillian. Not now," he protested, but she drew him into the bedroom. After, a lusty encounter, Bud was furious with himself. He had determined, on his way to her apartment, this would not happen – yet by God, he had given in.

Throwing on jeans and a t-shirt, Jillian returned to warm up a rotisserie chicken. They sat at the small kitchen table, saying little, sipping wine from a bottle of Chianti, leftover from a previous evening. Suddenly over the last of the bones on his plate, Bud laid down his fork and regarded her seriously.

"Hey, Jillian," Bud started slowly. "I have to tell you something."

She froze. His face was so clouded.

"This has got to be the last time."

"The last time for what?"

"You know…for this." His hand made a circle over the plates on the table, and included the bedroom door. "The whole…arrangement."

Jillian was silent.

Then he said, "This is the last time."

"You repeat yourself," she said, her voice choked.

"I'm getting married."

Jillian burst into tears.

"Sorry, Jillian. I don't mean to hurt you, but you know what we've been having is fun and games. It was never serious."

Jillian could not stop sobbing. "Maybe to you...not serious," she blubbered.

"You've known it," he said, growing concerned. "I never promised you anything. I thought you understood. We were great together in bed – but that was it."

"We were more than 'great' in bed...weren't we... just minutes ago?" she whimpered, arm pointed at the bedroom. "Right there... time and time again...and now you suddenly tell me we're through?"

"That part's always been fine," he said, trying to cajole her, "but what else did we ever do together? Did we ever go out to dinner? Did we ever go to the movies?"

"We ate lunch sometimes," she said. "I made you dinner..."

"Yeah, but we were never out in public. Always right here, next to your bedroom," he said with a grimace.

"What's the matter with that?"

"Nothing. Listen, you're a great girl..." he said, rising and approaching her on her side of the table. Bud sounded calm, but inside, he was riddled with nerves.

"I'm not a girl. I'm a woman," she said, sullen.

"OK. Woman. You'll find someone, I'm sure. But you've got to realize that this is it. I'm to be married and that's that." He was met with silence. He paused, looking at her, crumpled in her chair. "I'm sorry but I just can't do this anymore...Hey, you knew it was coming..." Then, in a low voice, he asked, "Did I ever say 'I love you'?"

"I saw it in your eyes."

"No! You saw lust."

Jillian stood up abruptly, her face hard. "I know who she is," she said, under her breath. "Of course I know. You've made no pretense of hiding your obsession."

"You know?" He was surprised, thrown off guard.

"You've got to be kidding. God, I've been having breakfast with her often enough…little Miss Muffet…little blonde girl who looks like a child."

"I can assure you she's no child, Jillian" Bud exclaimed. "She's the most responsive woman I have ever been with," this said pointedly, as he grabbed his jacket and headed for the door.

"You're leaving?" she shrieked.

"You bet."

"You're going to her?"

Bud did not answer, as Jillian leapt up and rushed toward him, embracing him from behind. Bud stiffened, in a state of raw panic. She was holding him so tight. She was desperate, hoping against hope that he would stay. He unclasped her arms about him and turned to her.

"What's the matter with you, Jillian?" His voice was gruff.

"Love, Bud. That's all. Love."

He moved away from her as quickly as he could, watching her face. It was twisted and flushed, her hair disheveled.

"You bastard!" she yelled. "You bastard. Be careful, fella. Better keep your gun close. Watch your back! Hey, you never know…"

As he strode to his cop car, he could hear Jillian's strident voice, a chilling echo in his head that carried far into the rainy night and mingled with his own self-disgust.

## Chapter Seventeen

# BITTER, WRETCHED, SCORNED

Jillian Rose. Her dream. Gone forever. Her Rose Bud. No more! No more!

She called the Sheriff's Office and said she had a fever. Indeed she did, not of temperature but of anger and self-contempt, a real sickness. She told her boss she did not know how long she'd be away from her job – "depending on when the fever breaks."

"Get yourself to a doctor, Jill, and do feel better." The Sheriff rang off, leaving Jillian stewing in the fact that 'the fever will never break. Never!'

In spite of the emotional hangover from his last night with Jillian, as Bud Rose sat in his cruiser, patrolling Westhampton Beach, he decided the wedding should be on the beach, in front of the monumental Atlantic Ocean. It was so fitting for his starfish, his Violet. To make her his wife with the ocean as witness seemed to Bud the perfect crown for his bride.

Underneath all his ruminations was another vision – of a brunette woman crumpled in a chair. He was sorry for Jillian. He had never meant to cause her pain. He knew that her father had left the family when Jillian was 10 years old, leaving her mother to raise the only child alone.

He knew it had been tough for Jillian. She had done well in high school, with many girl friends but few boys were interested in her lanky form. Little did they realize, Bud thought, that the tall young woman with the extra long legs was a gymnast in bed. Bud had to smile, but quickly sobered up when he thought of the hurt he had caused.

"Should I send a note and some flowers?" he said out loud. "Nah. It would only give her ideas. Leave well enough alone," and he gunned his car across the draw bridge to Dune Road, passing the Annas' stilt house, honking happily as he went by, and deciding the wedding would take place right there on the beach before Violet's first home.

Still early morning, Jillian went back to bed. Where else should she be but in the bed of lost love, she thought, burying her face in the pillow that smelled of him and drowning in tears? She stayed there most of the day

Toward evening, rising, stumbling into the kitchen area to make tea (to which she added a good slug of scotch, Bud's favorite), she sat at the table looking at the dried bones of last night's chicken on the two plates. She poured herself another slug, and with the swipe of her hand, she swept the plates crashing to the floor.

And suddenly, self-pity was gone. The tears were gone. Only anger remained, a burning desire to avenge her loss of love against the two in question. Bud Rose. Violet Annas.

"You are my enemies for life," she vowed out loud. "This ain't over, buster." She drank the scotch, now, directly from the bottle. "Just wait and see, Miss Pretty Little Slut! Jillian Burns is more than your equal. I am going to see to it that never, never, never will you live 'happily ever after'!"

Jillian started to laugh, rose and walked into the bedroom and passed out cold.

## Chapter Eighteen

# A WEDDING BY THE SEA

It was a July afternoon at 4:00 o'clock that Bud Rose married Violet Annas, a day exactly two years after ticketing her for speeding on Riverhead Road. It was also Violet's 22nd birthday.

She wore a long white silk charmeuse gown with a lace skirt overlay, the golden starfish pinned at her waist. Pink flowers in her hair, attached to a tiny veil, matched the pink sandals on her feet.

Bud was in a tuxedo with a white jacket and violet bow tie.

They stood at the edge of the water in front of George Annas' house under a cloudless sky, beside a silvery sea. The ceremony was brief, and attended by George, who gave the bride away, and Anastasia Annas. Joe Rose, Bud's Fireman father, who also worked in construction, and wife Alice who had a small seamstress business, stood there together, silent, happy. Bud's sister, Josie, who was married to the owner of the liquor store on Mill Road, John Cassidy, was Violet's matron of honor.

Sasha Annas was Bud's Best Man.

There were few, other than family: Bethany Brandeis, Violet's boss at the realtor's office, in a bright red sun dress, accompanied by her attorney, Mel Haddock, with a flower in his buttonhole; and two policemen, friends of Bud, and their wives. That was all.

The reception was held at The Patio, the back section of the restaurant cordoned off for the wedding party. Lavish hors d'oeuvres were passed by young waiters in long white aprons; shrimp and crab cakes, crudités with sauce, hot cheese puffs. And of course glasses of champagne on silver trays circulated among the guests. (There was the bar available for those of a stronger persuasion).

Here, more people were in attendance than at the wedding; The Sheriff; the Annas family physician (who had delivered Violet 22 years ago), Dr. Remsen and his wife Marie; the Reverend who had presided over the beach ceremony; Jordan Mather and his wife, from Quogue, casual friends of George (and owners of the green Ford bought at auction two years ago at the East End Hospice Gala); plus three or four more police officers and their girl friends.

Also, Jillian Burns appeared alone, in a white off-the-shoulder peasant blouse and brightly patterned skirt to the floor. It was a bold move on her part, as she had not been invited. She wore a false face of delight at the party for all to see. Inside, it was different: dark, jealous, almost unhinged.

Then she saw the Best Man, Sasha. They gravitated one to the other, because, inside Sasha, there was the same, dark, jealous, and unhinged turmoil torturing him too.

Bud stayed close to his bride for the entire time, enjoying the claps on the back, the congratulations, the exclamations. He did not acknowledge Jillian Burns in any way – no 'hello' – no nothing.

"How lovely your girl is," and "Where are you off to for your honeymoon, you lucky guy?" were exclamations by several of the male guests; "You sly fellow," this said with a thumbs up. Violet basked in Bud's adoration and the admiration of others.

From the corner of her eyes, she noticed Sasha and Jillian Burns huddled together at a table at the far edge of the room. What a pair! They looked sullen, but it was an expression Violet was used to in Sasha. He often wore that look, although in recent years, she had noticed he had grown more handsome than one would have thought possible. He had also learned to wear a façade of charm and grace that hid his vicious feelings.

But why so somber tonight – of all nights?

'It's my wedding night! You'd think he'd be glad to be rid of me. Now, he'll have Dad's house to himself with no competition!' Violet mused to herself.

Suddenly, she found it odd that a 31-year-old man would still live with mother and dad.

That was Sasha's problem. Tonight was Violet's night with her new husband. They planned to drive to the Islip-MacArthur airport in Violet's red coupe and stay at the Holiday Inn there for the night, then continue on into New York City the next day to The Mark Hotel on East 77th Street for an air-conditioned, sophisticated three-day visit to Gotham.

Violet had tickets for the Radio City Music Hall Show. She had booked dinner reservations at The Twenty-One Club for Saturday night, and had seats on the sightseeing boat from Battery Park in lower Manhattan that day-tripped around the island, planned for Sunday.

The rest of the time, she expected to remain in bed.

She was quite sure Bud would be willing to join her there. Oh yes. A more eager young husband was yet to be invented. How lucky she felt. How blessed.

She had to laugh. For her mini-honeymoon, she had wanted something different – away from sand and beach and sea gulls. And what did she plan? To go to another island, Manhattan, as engirded by water as Long Island, and book a ferryboat ride on those same waves.

I can't escape, she thought. The sea is part of me.

# Chapter Nineteen
# A DUBIOUS PAIRING

There was no coupling more dubious than the Sasha/Jillian connection. Yet, together, they had a common goal – to thwart the happiness of Violet and Bud; for Sasha, who had always hated his young sister for depriving him of his father's love – or so it seemed to him - through her diminutive beauty and feminine wiles; for Jillian, who held the passionate desire to alienate and send packing the pretty young woman from Bud Rose's arms and return him to her own.

For Jillian, there was a deeper, sinister motive as well: to see Bud bereft, to punish him in his heart as he had punished her, to see him drooling with lost lust, lost love.

Sasha and Jillian had known each other at the Westhampton Beach High School. They were in different grades, he two years older than she. Bud Rose had been a student too, the class above hers. Bud literally never noticed her at that time. Sasha, of course, being the oldest, ignored both younger students, and felt far superior.

Jillian had noticed Sasha at school during his final year there. But like Bud Rose, in those days, Sasha did not reciprocate. Besides, he was busy with Maryanne in the locker room. In later days, after Jillian acquired the job at the Sheriff's Office and became involved with Bud Rose, Jillian would see Sasha Annas in passing, as he was working at King Kullen, and her apartment was just down the street.

As time went by, Sasha had ascended, through the meat department, through the deli section, finally to assistant manager. The job came with an office to the side of the enormous aisled space within the King Kullen supermarket in Eastport.

Here, behind a glassed wall with pass through windows, he handled money. (He had learned his lesson after the camera incident.) Sasha cashed checks for customers, counted up the take for the day. He felt important in this role.

One of King Kullen's regular customers was Jillian Burns. After all, the store could not be more convenient, so she saw Sasha frequently, to nod to in passing, even to exchange an occasional pleasantry.

"What are the specials today," she would say coyly.

"Ask the butcher," would be the curt response.

Or, "You're lookin' good today, Sasha."

"You too, Jillian," he would answer, distractedly.

She noticed he had grown better looking with time, more presentable. But of course, she was mad for Bud Rose, so any romantic thoughts of Sasha – well they just did not exist.

After the Violet/Bud wedding reception, where Jillian and Sasha had sat together at a Patio table in their separate miseries, the two proceeded to the Triangle Pub for grilled cheese sandwiches and vodka on the rocks.

There, with the help of the liquor, they were able to express the raging grievances the incidence of slights and imagined cruelties that bedeviled the pair.

As the evening wore on, Jillian and Sasha made a pact.

"Let's split them apart," she announced. "We'll cut them in two – make them separate, alone, unhappy."

"You sound like you're ready to take an axe," Sasha said with a grin.

"Not a bad idea!"

"The only problem is," said Sasha, "they seem to be really in love."

"Hah!" Jillian almost shouted. "That Violet doesn't even know what love means. Now, Bud and I..." But she couldn't finish the sentence.

"You had a 'thing'?" Sasha questioned.

"A 'thing'?" Jillian answered, outraged. "A 'thing'? My God, we were madly in love."

Sasha looked at this half-inebriated, semi-pretty, angry woman and thought 'no way' but he did not say anything. Compared to his sister, and knowing Bud Rose, the very idea of Jillian Burns and Bud was unthinkable.

"Look," he said, trying to calm his companion. "They're off and running in a new marriage. Believe me, I'd love to see it crash. My sister has been a thorn in my side my whole life long!"

"My goodness! What's that, Sasha? Self-pity? Poor little Sasha." She grimaced.

It was his turn to get angry. "Just a minute, Jillian. I am more than ready to see a miserable ending for the two of them. But how? Just what do you suggest?" he said with a sneer.

"Don't you dare underestimate me, Sasha. I have a secret. I'm biding my time. Just wait and see. And when the moment of truth comes, I hope you're with me. I swear I'm going to make them suffer."

"You can count me in," Sasha said, somehow convinced that it was possible. "It's a deal," and he took her limp hand and shook it. "Come on. I'll get you home," and Sasha did. He spent the night in her bed, the two of them so out of it, nothing happened to make the bed bounce, nothing at all.

## Chapter Twenty

# THE LITTLE HOUSE ON SHORE ROAD

The 1ˢᵗ of August, Bud and Violet moved into a little house on the bay in Remsenburg, a hamlet west of Westhampton Beach. It was at the very end of Shore Road, with the view of the dunes across the water of Moriches Bay. There were reeds in front of the single story house that grew quite marshy during high tide, but Bud and Violet knew when to avoid those reeds with their bare feet.

Violet had gotten them a sweet deal in the purchase of the house because of her involvement with Brandeis Realty. She was smart enough to realize that her boss, Bethany Brandeis, was eager to obtain a listing for sale of Violet's father's stilt house on the ocean near The Swordfish Club on Dune Road, an immensely valuable piece of land (Forget the house! That could be replaced.)

In consequence, Bethany was very 'forgiving' of Violet's situation and of the fact that the newly married couple had a limited budget. By making their purchase so attractive, she hoped to soften up Violet sufficiently to help the realtor weaken the resistance of Violet's father.

"Consider the low interest I arranged for your mortgage at the bank a partial wedding present," Bethany had said with a smile at the closing. "And as for the overall price, you know I could have gotten a great deal more for it."

"I realize that, Ms. Brandeis," Bud had piped up. "We don't ask for any favors, but we sure do appreciate…"

"Call me Bethany," the realtor interrupted, eyeing the handsome police officer with a studied admiration. "My pleasure, Bud…if I may call you that."

"You may, indeed, Bethany," he replied, almost blushing. "But really, our thanks."

The deal was done.

On the August day, when they moved into the two-bed-room house, with its sunny front room, Bud set up a new TV on a table opposite the open kitchen area. "There's no way that TV is going into the bedroom, my sweet!" he declared. "Not in front of the 'work bench,'" a name he had for their large, double bed. "I want no distractions…just you and me."

Actually, it took very little 'work' to please Violet. She was a naturally juicy young woman and was crazy in love with her husband. With the gentle breeze through the windows, open to the bay, with the moon lighting their room of love with a glow, life for the two was indeed "La Vie En Rose."

Later that summer month, Bud Rose transferred to the Riverhead Police Department. He was a Detective at this point in his career, and although his police car (different plates) was still his mode of transport, his duties at the RPD were more complex.

He had asked for the transfer for a highly personal reason: Jillian Burns. Her immediacy in the Westhampton Beach Sheriff's office and her depressing proximity to her old lover made him uncomfortable. He couldn't stand it. The black mood in the office that emanated directly from her desk was sour, and the baleful looks and pointed remarks that were sent his way he found disgusting.

"You got a hickey on your neck," she'd blurt out in a loud voice. "The price of being married?" she'd say with a little snicker.

Bud would wince and exit the premises as fast as he could.

"Oh, oh, cop. There's a long blonde hair on your lapel. Somebody's little head on your shoulder, eh?"

Jillian couldn't help herself. Some of those early August days were better than others, but when she saw Bud, entering the office with such a bounce in his step and huge grin on his face, her words would tumble out, direct from her heart, in spite of herself.

For Bud, the new gig in Riverhead for the RPD was a great relief. His office was on Howell Avenue. The town of Riverhead, on the Peconic River, was the County seat of Suffolk County, and the police department was large in comparison to that of Westhampton Beach. The pay was much higher than the statewide average. Bud was pulling down near $75,000 per year. As a newlywed, this made him proud before his bride.

"Wow, darling!" Violet exclaimed. "Didn't know I was marrying a rich man!" And Violet would embrace him, and the little house became the lovely cocoon of which he had always dreamed. Life could not have been better.

He loved his new position which provided a new challenge that he relished. As Detective Rose, he was placed in the Special Problems Unit of the RPD, which separated him out from the usual home invasion, drug busts, thefts and drag strip duties that the town experienced – normal activities for the regular police units.

His first and truly intense duty was in trying to break a case of expensive car thefts that plagued the East End. Porches, Mercedes, Maseratis, and the like, were being stolen from the expensive mansions and high priced restaurant parking lots, all the length of the East End of Long Island from Eastport to Montauk Point. These vehicles were presumably to be shipped and sold elsewhere. It was obvious that one person could not possibly do this alone. A gang worked this criminal cartel of sorts, and it was Bud's job to track down and arrest the perps, a big job worthy of his large salary.

Just where were these vehicles taken and how were they kept, unnoticed, until they could be moved to a place of purchase? And how were they moved?

It was a puzzle he brought home with him at night, but quickly set aside. His delightful bride was waiting for him with something delicious to eat on the table, a newly opened bottle of Pinot Noir, and that radiant smile on her face. His RPD tasks were done for the day. The 'work bench' was awaiting for the night.

# Chapter Twenty-One

# POLISH TOWN

Bud performed other duties for the RPD, while working on his major theft case. As a police detective new to the community, he was sent to patrol the annual Polish Town Fair, which opened for two days on Saturday, August 20th. He first moved about slowly in his cop car on the Riverhead streets, then on foot. He was there to protect against any petty crime or offense that might take place. And, of course, with gun on his hip, he was also prepared for more serious encounters.

The Polish Town Fair had taken place for a number of years, a great moment for the large contingent of Polish people who had flocked to the town of Riverhead at the beginning of the last century. It celebrated their heritage and was always presided over by Miss Polish Town, a local beauty who was selected in a pageant, earlier in the spring.

Bud, now walking Pulaski Street, the heart of Polish Town, was startled to see Sasha Annas buying two kielbasa sandwiches at one of the stands set up on the sidewalk. The air was filled with Polka music and a carnival atmosphere prevailed. There were more stands with pierogies, and other polish delicacies to eat, fragrant in the sunshine.

Bud found it strange to find his brother-in-law at such an event. It was so uncharacteristic of the rather taciturn, up-tight Sasha to be in a festive, relaxed atmosphere such as the Polish Town Fair. And he was with a girl who was bent over her sausage sandwich.

He approached the couple. Sasha looked almost offended at the appearance of Bud. "What are you doing here?" Sasha asked abruptly.

"I'm working the fair, what else?" responded Bud.

"Oh. I see," said Sasha. He seemed repentant of his rudeness. Bud was looking at the girl who had lifted her head, her long printed caftan sweeping the pavement.

Bud lost his breath.

"This is Jillian," Sasha said, introducing her to the cop.

"Having a good time?" Bud managed to ask.

"Yes," she replied, dimpling as she gave him the once-over. Her look was not lost on Sasha. He was not pleased.

"Surprised to see you here, Sasha," Bud remarked.

"Why?"

"Well, it's not your usual gig – at least that's what I assume."

"You assumed wrong," and with that, Sasha took Jillian's arm. She grinned at Bud with a large wink. They walked away from the policeman who stood watching them move quickly through the crowd. He followed them after a minute. Farther down Pulaski Street, they turned into The Birchwood of Polish Town, a bar known for its tough clientele, and according to local police gossip, often the place for late-night fights.

What the hell was Sasha doing with Jillian? Bud hadn't seen her for a few weeks, hadn't even thought of her. And a bar before noon? Maybe drinks at The Birchwood was a necessity for the pair.

Bud did not realize that Sasha was a regular at the place and had certain 'friends' who frequented The Birchwood as often as he. One of them was Jillian; another, a guy named Vinny from New York City; a third, a young Polish fellow named Tadeusz, (called Tad by his buddies) who worked as a sous-chef in a restaurant all the way out in Greenport on the North Fork; and then there was Willie Yablonski, a mechanic at George Annas' Ford dealership on Montauk Highway in Westhampton Beach.

The five had become close and would sit at a round table in the back room of The Birchwood, drinking vodka and 'talking', if you could call it that. More like plotting!

Money. Big money was the focus of their conversation. They all craved it. They could taste the dollars.

"From the fat cats," Vinny said. "You know, the summer millionaires who arrive from Memorial Day to Labor Day."

"Oh, they're still coming down for Thanksgiving and Christmas too, not just mid-summer," Jillian piped up. "I babysit a lot of evenings during the holidays."

"So it's open season, eh?" Vinny said with a sly look. "All year long except maybe mid-winter. We're in business, right?"

"Right!" was the chorus of answers. "Skoal!"

# Chapter Twenty-Two

# EAST MORICHES

Jillian Burns was pregnant! It was her secret. No one knew.

She discovered the fact shortly after Bud Rose broke off with her the previous spring, at the time of his engagement to Violet. By July, at the time of the Rose wedding, Jillian was just over three months along.

Although uninvited, Jillian had boldly attended the Patio reception after Bud and Violet's ceremony on the beach. Jillian dressed carefully in a long peasant skirt. Being tall, there had been no obvious sign of her condition..

She had decided the baby would be part of a long-term plan, a malevolent one she concocted and relished, embroidering all manner of mischief and pain for the two who walked away in their short-lived haze of happiness. Jillian would see to it that their 'love' would not last. She and the baby she carried would burst that bubble.

As August progressed, as Jillian's body grew with her pregnancy and started to show, people began to say to her, "Gained a pound or two, Jillian?" said with a chuckle. She decided to move in with her mother at her house in East Moriches, not far from Westhampton Beach. On September 1st, she quit her job at the Sheriff's Office, telling her boss that her mother needed her, that she had to take care of her, that "Mom has the early signs of Alzheimer disease," an absolute lie.

Of course, Stella Burns had no such ailment. But she worried about her daughter, particularly after Jillian revealed she was pregnant. Mrs.

Burns was more than ready to take her in, although she disapproved of the whole situation about which Jillian told her nothing.

"Who got you this way?"

"None of your business, Mom."

"Any chance he'll marry you?" this asked cautiously.

"Maybe one day. In due time." And Jillian would change the subject.

As for Sasha, Jillian had told him she was leaving town for a new job. "Better pay," she explained. Their goodbye, though sexually active, was unsentimental. Sasha did not even ask where she was going.

Fortunately, Mrs. Burns had saved her money. She had worked as an accountant for a large firm in Riverhead. Now retired, she not only had her pension, but Social Security, Medicare, a good supplemental health insurance plan, and had invested wisely outside of her IRA. Mrs. Burns, for an elderly retired widow, was quite flush.

And Jillian was no slouch at protecting her own future financially. She was frugal in buying clothes, had been paying very low rent. Although she was bored to death in her mother's home and had serious morning sickness, as time moved on, she was grateful for the haven of the house in East Moriches and her mother's fussing over her.

"My first grandchild," Stella Burns would coo. "Don't you want to know the sex?"

"I couldn't care less."

East Moriches was a boon for Jillian. It was just far enough away from Westhampton Beach and her old haunts to give her cover. No one knew she was there. She was able to do her shopping for food at the local farms and grocery store. As her pregnancy made her more and more uncomfortable, her cumbersome size making movement difficult, her mother's home became a hidden lair.

It was as if Jillian Burns had disappeared from the region. Some were curious. Others did not care.

Only Sasha Annas truly registered her absence. "Why the hell she never even told me where she went," he complained to himself. "What about her grand plan to screw Bud Rose and Violet! I knew she was not to be trusted. She was all words!"

For this reason alone, Sasha noticed that Jillian was missing in action, but he did not miss her. That fact did not for one minute diffuse his own hostile feelings against his new brother-in-law and his benighted sister, Violet. His fury went deep. Like an ocean wave, he wanted to swallow Violet up, spit her out, and leave her, a starfish in the sand.

That would be justice, like the golden pin in the shape of a starfish that Violet wore at her throat or in her hair or in the folds of her dress. His sister would be cold on the damp shore and made of gold no more, her glitter gone, turning gray and lifeless.

# Chapter Twenty-Three

# TREES DOWN — WATER HIGH

Sitting at the table in the home on Shore Road eating shrimp in a spicy sauce, Violet felt a tingle. "Bud," she cried. "My feet are wet!"

The water was several inches across the floor. She could hear the wind deepening outside the house, as the sea rose. Hundreds of tidal creeks and marshes that threaded through Long Island brought saltwater into peoples' houses and killed the trees in fields and yards.

By midnight that evening in early October, the first Nor'Easter hit the East Coast and Long Island dead center. Bud and Violet were summarily evacuated by the Westhampton Beach Firemen, sloshing through the rising bay water and telling them to leave "NOW!"

The rains had come and the wind howled and the bay grew bloated as the uncontrollable Atlantic Ocean took over the outer dunes and the houses upon them. The wild water filled the well of Moriches Bay to bursting, and reached up Shore Road almost 3/4s of a mile.

So much for La Vie En Rose!

Violet and Bud managed to drive their car through the rising water on Shore Road to the main street of Remsenburg, just in time. They headed west toward the Long Island Expressway to find a place to sleep.

They drove through swirling clouds and sudden bursts of heavy rain, the wind nearly pulling the Ford red coupe off the road. Bud was determined, face set, as he guided the automobile as best he could.

Violet sat in the adjacent seat hugging herself, silent. Her thoughts could not help but return to those of the six-year-old little girl who had tried to rock herself to sleep, under her bunk bed and drown out the desperate voices. Now, all she heard was the wind, but the fear was there of water rising violently in her memory, and the sound of a child crying.

She looked at Bud. "I'm scared," she whispered.

"We're okay, darling. We'll be just fine," he said, although he was not sure he meant it.

Wherever they stopped, at every motel sign at points off the highway, they were turned away. The places were filled with evacuees.

Finally, just across from the Islip-MacArthur Airport, they found a rundown, wooden motel with rooms attached to each other in a long row. There was an 'Open' sign, and with relief, they were able to book a room with a lumpy bed, a decent bathroom, and shelter from the storm.

Wet and disconsolate, Bud and Violet sat side by side on the coverlet. Violet was trembling.

"You okay?" he asked kindly.

"Yeah," she said. "You?"

"As long as you are, I'm okay," said with a smile, and he took her in his arms.

The thin door was rattled by the wind throughout the night. Bud held her close. Her final words to him before she finally slept were, "I hope our house is still there."

"Why wouldn't it be?" he murmured.

"Because of the sea…the ocean could carry our little home all the way to China." Then, in a choked voice, "At least no one is inside."

She could hear his chuckle before sleep took her.

Bud and Violet's return to Shore Road on the morning after the October storm was fraught with danger. Large downed trees and power lines were blocking the roads as they drove east, from the Islip-MacArthur airport. Puddles of water – deep and dangerous –pocketed the byways leading towards Remsenburg. It took several hours to arrive at their extremely damp and rather pathetic looking home.

"It looks like it drowned," whimpered Violet as they drove into the back driveway.

"At least it's still there," Bud said. "And it's fixable. Don't worry."

Bud grabbed the small case they had brought with them to the motel and headed toward the house. The case contained bits of clothing and what they called an 'escape' folder. This included their birth certificates, insurance documents, the latest tax forms. Bud was an organized man, and Violet, too, planned ahead and followed the Girl Scout motto, 'Be Prepared'. It was her father's trait. He too anticipated events.

"One never knows what lies ahead," George Annas would expound to his family when she was little. This had stuck with her. Her father was particularly respectful of the ocean and its power, hence the love he had for the stilts. He had prepared for the sea's encroachment in advance by purchasing, in the early 50s, a little house on long legs.

This fact occurred to Violet as she left the car and walked on the mushy reeds to their house. The interior floors were wet with salt water, puddled in places and muddied as well. "This is disgusting," she exclaimed.

"It's going to be quite a job – Jeez!" Bud said, looking around, scratching his head. "I'm glad the TV is at least up on a table." At this moment, the phone rang. "Hey, that's amazing," Bud said.

"What?"

"That it works," and he picked up the receiver.

"You kids all right?" It was George Annas. "You weather the storm?"

"Yes sir, we did," replied Bud. "We managed to get a motel up near Islip. Made it back – but the damage to trees and stuff – it was brutal."

"I'm sure," said George. "How's your house? Did it survive?"

"You could say so. But, boy, it's a mess – water and mud inside. Violet doesn't look too happy," Bud said glancing at his wife who sat on the couch looking at her soaking wet sandals.

George laughed. "We're still here, high up in our little nest – one of the few houses left, from what I can see."

"Thank God for that," Bud responded.

"Thank God for stilts," George replied. "Hey, I have a suggestion. This could easily happen again – I mean a storm like this one. Why don't you have your house raised, not on stilts maybe, but put it on stanchions, above the high water line."

"Wouldn't that be expensive?"

"Not when you think of the next storm to come and the next. Every repair job will cost you. In the long run, it's worth considering. Besides, you'd have a great new view of the bay." George laughed again.

"Hmm. Makes sense."

"Just a suggestion, Bud. Think about it. My little house on stilts has survived many a storm – including hurricanes, over the years. Anyway, take care, you two. Gotta get you over for dinner soon," and he rang off.

Violet smiled for the first time that morning, when Bud told her of George's recommendation.

"You know, Dad's got a point. Let's do it, Bud. You're making more money since you transferred to the Riverhead Police Department, and I get Real Estate commissions from time to time. It makes great sense."

"You're right," he agreed.

"I love our little house – and we will be able to see across the bay and beyond and I love you, Mr. Cop," and with that, Violet approached Bud and put her arms about him and he lifted her and purposely carried her into the bedroom and laid her on the cool dry bed, where he went to 'work'.

# Chapter Twenty-Four

## STORAGE WAREHOUSE

For many weeks, Detective Bud Rose worked on the investigation into the nest of stolen car robbers who were creating a major problem for some wealthy East End homeowners. Even their guests could be prey. On two particular occasions, both happening the same night – Thanksgiving Night – of 1984 – in Southampton Village, a black Jaguar and a midnight blue Lamborghini, were taken separately from the driveways of two different houses on Halsey Neck Lane, north of the Atlantic beachfront. The outcry from the two visiting guest victims was vociferous and immediate, as was that from their hosts

Bud, as lead detective of the Special Unit Force of the RPD, worked closely with the Southampton Police Department. It was he who had a suspicion as to where the stolen cars were first taken, to be hidden away. It was a hunch, felt in his gut.

A large storage facility was located near the Suffolk County Air Base, off Riverhead Road as it led north out of Westhampton Beach. The various connected, metal enclosed sheds were rented to individuals who housed their possessions within. Most of the clients were home owners who left summer outdoor furniture, steamer trunks, even small Boston Whaler boats and surf boards in their leased storage sheds for the winter.

Bud Rose decided it could be a prime spot to hide stolen vehicles, each one in its own little separate garage. He kept the storage facility in his eye, every day, watching carefully the comings and goings of people storing their belongings for the winter.

One day in early December, he saw a man drive into the place in a spiffy Mercedes Benz, followed by another car, a Toyota. Bud followed the two automobiles in his cruiser. The guy, in the Mercedes, when he got out of the car, had on jeans and a ratty t-shirt, appearing not to be a rich man, although Bud knew looks could be deceptive.

The man went into the office, presumably to pay for and secure a storage shed, as the Toyota, driven by a young woman, waited. The man was in the office for a few moments. On returning to his Mercedes, he drove down the line of units, stopped at number 17, opened the metal door with a key, and drove the car inside. Bud saw there was plenty of room.

Bud parked and approached the man as he was closing the storage room door, locking it, ready to join the woman in the Toyota.

"Excuse me, sir," Bud said.

"What's up, officer?" the man asked.

"Yes, well, I'm investigating a case involving an automobile and I saw you coming in here…"

"Look, officer," the man said respectfully. "I've heard about a number of thefts out here on the East End, but I can assure you, this isn't one of them. I'm leaving my car here for the winter – no need for it in the city. Should be safe here. Look. Here's my registration…my license…I can…"

"No need," Bud said. "Sorry to have bothered you." And he bid his goodbye, got back in the cruiser and left the premises.

Bud parked at the back of the Suffolk County Air Base (a facility that protected the city of New York in case of attack) and sat in his car for a moment. The man was straight. Bud was sure, but what an ideal place to hide an automobile from view.

Bud figured the expensive automobiles could be secreted, each separately, for some time, then driven, perhaps in the dead of a winter's night, to Orient Point, the eastern most town on the North Fork of Long Island. There, the vehicles could be driven onto the Orient Point early morning ferry, cross Long Island Sound, arriving in New London,

Connecticut, where they could be sold or sent to different locations around New England – or even shipped abroad from the port of New London.

Bud had been working the case all through the fall and well into the Christmas season. Winter would be different as the East End kind of dropped dead. People stayed in New York City, did not usually care to drive on the icy roads and snow of the colder months.

It would be the perfect time to ferry the vehicles, perhaps one by one, across the Sound - with so few visitors and tourists around, only locals absorbed in their circumscribed lives.

Thefts were still continuing, as the New Year began, the latest from a house in Quogue. It was the Mather mansion built in the early 1900s, on the bay side of Dune Road near the Quogue Beach Club (an old stamping ground of Bud and Violet where they had made love on the sand).

The place belonged to the large family that had summered there for all those years. The huge living room had a stone fireplace at each end. There was still no heating system, but when those hearths were burning high, the center of the house was comfortable.

It was a wealthy enclave. This particular New Year's Eve weekend, there were several cars in the circular driveway at the entrance of the Mather property. One of them was a brand new silver Corvette, a Christmas present for Rodney Mather, the youngest son. The young man had already placed Vanity Plates saying 'Hottest Rod' on his prized new possession.

Next to it was parked the pedestrian green Ford Jordan Mather had bought at the East End Hospice Gala two summers earlier. There was also a Dodge sedan and a Toyota on the gravel.

It was cold this early New Year's Eve morning, when Rodney went to the driveway to whisk into town in his glorious new automobile. He discovered that the place on the grass, off the driveway where he had parked, only showed tire tread traces.

No car!

Well! Rodney let out a yelp loud enough to raise the whole household. Three young men in stages of undress, holiday visitors, (one never knew exactly who and how many were staying in the large house) came running to Rodney's side. His father, Jordan, soon ambled out, holding a coffee cup.

"Well I'll be damned," he remarked. "What'd you do, Rod? Leave it at some bar in Southampton last night?"

"No way. It was right here, wasn't it guys?" the son said, turning to his friends. "You know it was!" Rodney was beside himself with anger, and ready to cry with loss.

"Yes, sir. It was here, Mr. Mather. We came home in it last night," this said in a chorus of boyish voices.

"I guess we better call the cops." And Jordan Mather returned to the living room of the house and did just that.

When he came back to the driveway and the buzzing young men, he announced that the Sheriff was calling the Riverhead Police Department (RPD) because they were investigating a number of thefts of valuable cars on the whole East End.

"A detective from the RPD Special Units will be over – probably by noon. So, boys, prepare yourselves to be questioned," and Jordan Mather went back inside to resume his breakfast.

The RPD detective who arrived near the lunch hour was Bud Rose.

"Did you boys hear anything last night…a car door slam…feet on the gravel…?" This was Bud's opening question to the group of four. They were all standing on the driveway.

"We were kind of out of it…been partying…you know, and of course, when it must have happened, we were inside," said Rodney.

"Couldn't hear anything out here," mumbled another boy with red hair.

"What time did you get home from Southampton?"

The four looked from one to the other. "Dunno," said Rodney. "Must have been close to 3:00." They all nodded.

Bud had gotten the Vanity Plate number. He probed the four hung-over young men, getting no information that might help. There was little in the form of clues. Bud did take photos of the tire treads. He also took the Corvette's registration number (still in Rodney's wallet) and his driver's license number. There was little else to be done. As he left in his cruiser, he could only think the theft of such an automobile was almost impossible to trace – but a flashy silver car...pretty conspicuous. Someone just might have spotted it. He put the cruiser in gear and headed for the storage complex out by the airport. The office was closed.

# Chapter Twenty-Five
## SASHA/JILLIAN

"Why would a 31-year old man still live at home? Don't you want your independence?" Jillian asked with a lascivious wink.

"Why wouldn't a 3l-year old man live at home if the rent was free, his hot meals cooked – no King Kullen grocery costs there – and his clothes washed and pressed on a daily basis? Makes sense to me. And as far as 'independence' is concerned, I'm pretty 'independent' in seeing whomever and whatever I please," Sasha replied, eyeing the naked woman next to him.

Jillian had returned from East Moriches to her rental (month to month) opposite King Kullen when the baby was still tiny, leaving her in her mother's home. The two adult women had grown testy as the days had passed since the child's birth.

She began looking for a job in the Westhampton Beach area where they had day care. It was impossible to find. She settled for a position as receptionist at the Storage Warehouse near the Suffolk County Air Base. The pay was not bad, and she convinced her mother to keep the baby, paying her a small fee and visiting the little girl on weekends.

The first person she contacted on returning to her apartment in Eastport near King Kullen was Sasha Annas. It was early January 1985. He was strangely incurious about her recent disappearance from the community, but he returned to her bouncing bed with alacrity.

Her feelings for Sasha were tepid at best, but he was a vigorous man and for the moment, that was what mattered to her...athletic sex. It made her forget lost love, true desire, at least while it was happening.

Jillian made no mention of her daughter, that she had given birth to a child at 8:30 PM, on December 6th, 1984, in the hospital in Riverhead. Sasha had no idea, although he commented on the larger size of her breasts on more than one occasion. "What you been doing to pump these up?" he had remarked. "I like it. I like it a lot!"

Of course, the aftermath of Sasha's sexual ministrations to her body was for Jillian, a sense of terrible devastation. No one, no amount of excitement could ease that bereft feeling, no matter how intense the coupling had been.

Bud Rose was gone from her, but hardly forgotten. He was remembered, not with love, but with a pervasive bitterness that could not be denied. And there was the baby! Jillian's feelings for her little one were ambivalent, unemotional. When first realizing she was pregnant, she had considered an immediate abortion.

Instead, she decided the child was the ultimate weapon.

As the Sasha/Jillian connection continued, in their evenings in The Birchwood in Riverhead, and their encounters in bed, she began to resent Sasha.

He was not Bud Rose.

"Go home, Sasha," she would say. "Go back to Mommie Dearest in your silly house on the dunes. She cooks your meals and presses your clothes like you were still 10 years old! That's where you belong. Not here," and she would turn over in the bed until he left.

On his way out, he would exclaim, "I thought you were going to do a dirty deed against your old lover and his air-head bride. Remember, you were ready to take an axe? What's happened to all that venom? Now, you seem to be directing it at me!" And he would slam the door.

After Sasha's bitter departing words, Jillian would sit up enraged and shout to the walls of her room, "You're just another bastard, Sasha Annas. Just another creep in my life, and don't worry, my mean little friend, Bud Rose will pay and your pathetic little sister will get what's coming to her. Vengeance is mine!"

# Chapter Twenty-Six

## SURPRISE

Bud pulled into the office parking lot of the Storage Warehouse out near the Suffolk County Air Base, after 5:00 in the afternoon on a mid-January Wednesday.

He entered the small office through its half-glass front door and was surprised to see, sitting at the front desk, Jillian Burns!

She looked up with a coy smile and said, "Well. Hello, Mr. Cop? What can I do for you?"

"Hey, Jillian." Bud was staggered.

"Saw each other at the Polish Day event in August," she purred?"

"You were with Sasha Annas," Bud said stiffly.

"That's right. We're friends." There was a pause. "What's up?"

"I've been wondering about this…" Bud waved his hand around the office.

"This is the office. What's to wonder about?"

"It's not just the office," Bud said. "I'm talking about the whole facility. For instance, how many units do you have to rent?"

"One hundred ten. Why?"

Bud ignored the question. "Are the rentals mostly seasonal or are there people who keep them yearly on a regular basis?"

"We have both. Look, Mr. Cop, I've got to be closing."

"Just a few more questions." Bud said this firmly because he had noticed Jillian was suddenly nervous with his probing and eager to escape his scrutiny.

95

"For instance," he continued, "do renters just come and go at will? I mean do they have to come to the office every time they take something out of their individual unit or put something into it?" He was struggling to sound professional.

"I don't understand," Jillian said, busy with adjusting papers on the desk.

"Sure you do." Bud paused. "Do they have to check with you…with the office… when they move something in or out?"

"No, of course not. Once they have a contract with us, they are free to come and go. They can do whatever they want. They each have a key to their particular unit."

"So," Bud mused. "Is the facility full? Are all the units taken?"

"Why? You want one?" she said, standing behind the desk, hand on hip.

"No. I don't want one, but if I did, are there any available." Bud was growing disgusted.

"Yes. Let me look," and Jillian bent over and looked at the computer screen. "Yes. We have numbers 79 and 80, available and then there are two of the double size units left– numbers 101 and 102 – These two can even be thrown together if need be."

"Does that ever happen?"

"It happens with large racing boats… even a sail boat – with its mast down, of course. A Boston Whaler size can fit into the regular unit, but for anything larger, it would take two units."

"How many double size units are there…out of the whole one hundred-ten?"

Jillian peered at the computer screen again. "There are15." She closed the top of the computer, picked up her purse, hanging on the back of her desk chair and walked around to stand beside Bud, her face upturned. "Is that all, Mr. Cop?"

"For now," Bud said abruptly, and turned and left through the front door.

Jillian's face collapsed. She sank into the chair by her desk. Through clenched teeth, she whispered, "He'll come around again, and when he does, I'll be waiting."

## Chapter Twenty-Seven

# DEAD OF WINTER

The winter of 1985 on Long Island opened cold and icy. The surface of roads and highways were hard and slippery. Snow coated the trees and lay heavy on the telephone wires that laced the island.

Bud Rose was determined to pursue the auto thieves. Like a bloodhound, his nose was raised and acutely sensitive. He was sure in his gut that the summer auto robberies – some of the cars themselves, at least – were still on Long Island, waiting to be driven away, with the winter itself as cover. And his instinct about the Storage Warehouse beat like a pulse at his wrist.

He avoided going into the office because of the new receptionist, Jillian Burns!

However, a day did not go by that he did not case the place, and as the frigid days continued, he would, at least once a week, drive to the Suffolk County Air Base at midnight. The Storage Warehouse would loom darker than the darkness and exhibit no activity. But this did not discourage him. There was something there, he was convinced.

"Drive carefully, sweetheart," Violet would whisper as he climbed out of their warm bed. He would reassure her. "Don't worry. Go back to sleep."

It was a slow period at the Real Estate Office. Few people were looking at summer properties or homes on the beach as February, March progressed. It would take the whisper of spring in the air to bring buyers and renters out from the city to explore the properties listed at Brandeis Realty.

Yet, it was the kind of laid-back time when the Bud Rose's could have cement stanchions built – four of them – under the corners of their home on Shore Road in Remsenburg. The house was lifted up almost eight feet, giving the young owners a grand view across Moriches Bay. They were so pleased, they added a front deck – small but inviting – with wicker chairs set out and a little coffee table.

"It will be so delightful when spring finally comes," Violet cooed. "We can sit and watch the sunsets and drink our red wine and watch the birds."

"Lovely thought, darling," said Bud, beaming. "We can ask your Dad and Anastasia to join us. It was his idea to catch the view."

During the winter, George Annas had joined the movie theater Movie Club. For a $100 membership, he and guest could attend the movies shown at the Movie Club, mostly older films, usually black and white classics and cult favorites from past years, like 'Psycho' and 'Citizen Kane' and 'Double Indemnity'.

George and Anastasia enjoyed these moving picture evenings. They had fallen in love at the Westhampton Beach Theater. So it was a natural fit that they join the Movie Club. Every Wednesday, through the winter months, they went promptly at 7:30 pm and sat in the balcony.

On more than one occasion, Violet and Bud joined them. Although not members, they were able to buy cut-rate tickets. Anastasia would have prepared a warming dinner of beef short ribs in gravy with mashed potatoes, or a braised chicken with lemons and olives, or a true Russian borscht with sour cream.

"Stick to the ribs food", George would say, as the four would sit at the table in the stilt house on the dunes. He would be happily downing the savory dinner. "It's almost 7:00," he would suddenly exclaim. "Don't want to miss a minute of tonight's feature... 'Casablanca'...my war, ya know." And they would be off, in separate cars.

Sasha was never in sight.

The winter months went by at a slow pace, with dreams of summer, Bud's midnight forays to the Storage facility, and gentle loving in the house on Shore Road.

# Chapter Twenty-Eight

# OPEN HOUSE – SPRING 1985

Springtime was about to arrive and when it did, Violet held her first Open House for a client of Brandeis Realty. It was on a Sunday, the 1st of April. The home for sale was a grand mansion on Basket Neck Lane in Remsenburg, listed at $1,400,00 – a tidy sum. The property had a large back lawn (with pool), an extraordinary master bedroom abutting it, and a state of the art kitchen.

Violet set up her 'For Sale' sign in the front driveway, opened the massive front door with a key, and placed her brochures on the rosewood table in the foyer. She had also brought a vase of white lilies to put on the Steinway grand piano in the living room. The owners, of course, were in New York City. The 'season' for them on the East End of Long Island had yet to begin – Memorial Day.

But 'lookers' were on the prowl on spring weekends. It was a busy time for realtors, perhaps the busiest time of the year.

Violet sat down at the mahogany desk in the living room. She did not want to rumple the throw pillows on the bright red couch that centered the room. She pulled out a book she was reading, a romance novel entitled "Love on the Beach." It was a silly story but anything to pass the time until a client arrived.

The first couple to come appeared near 2:00 o'clock in the afternoon. They were a plump, prosperous pair, dressed in Ralph Lauren sporty clothes and rather pompous in their demeanor.

"Not bad," the husband announced, looking at the piano, "if anyone knows how to play it."

"Oh sure," responded the wife. "Ginny, - she's our daughter" –this, said to Violet – "she's taking lessons."

"Yeah, but would she want to play on a summer's day?" said the man sardonically.

Violet was laying out the guest book for them to sign (with address and contact numbers), which they proceeded to do. 'Mr. and Mrs. Edward Conroy.'

"May I show you the master? It's over here to your right," Violet announced, and she led them to the superior bedroom bordering the garden and pool. She left the pair there, running to the entrance foyer where the bell had rung. Violet was astonished, on opening the door, to see Jillian Burns standing on the granite stoop.

She was wearing jeans and sneakers and around her chest was a wraparound cloth, a carrying blanket to house the infant it enclosed. Violet could see the top of a small head with light fuzzy hair.

"Good Lord, Jillian!" Violet exclaimed. "My goodness. What are you doing here?"

"May we come in?" Jillian asked, sweeping past Violet and entering the foyer.

"This is an Open House, Jillian, for a very expensive property, as you can see. Why did you stop by?"

"I saw your Ford coupe – your little red car – and I knew I'd find you here…it's been a long time. I wondered how you're doing."

"I'm fine…but I have some clients here to take care of." Violet could not stop looking at the baby's head.

"Oh, don't worry about me. I'll just wander about. My, this place IS grand, isn't it!" And with that, mother and child crossed the broad living room and looked out the back window toward the pool.

"You have a baby?" Violet exclaimed, her voice stumbling.

"Looks like I do, doesn't it," Jillian said over her shoulder, not turning to look at Violet who was stuck in the middle of the rug, mouth agape.

At this moment, the Conroy's appeared in the doorway. "Oh, we've got some competition, I see," Ed said, eyeing Jillian suspiciously.

"Oh, I'm just here to say hello to my friend Violet," Jillian responded.

"Okay. Good, because we really like the house…like it enough to probably make an offer. Price is high…are the owners flexible?" this said with a sidelong grin at Violet from Ed Conroy.

"We'll have to see about that, Mr. Conroy, when an offer is made…I do thank you for coming. It is a great house, isn't it? and what a delightful area – Basket Neck Lane – terrific neighbors – and…" Violet was showing them to the door.

"It's really quite perfect," Mrs. Conroy remarked.

"Now Gracie. Let's not overdo it." As the two went onto the driveway, Mr. Conroy called, "We'll be in touch."

Violet closed the door and as she turned in the foyer, she was startled to find Jillian directly in front of her.

"Well, I'll be going too, I guess. It is a fine house…wish I could afford it." She laughed. "Nice seeing you, Violet."

"The baby?" Violet couldn't help herself.

"Little girl," Jillian said.

"When? Did you…?"

"Marry?" Jillian finished the question. "No, no need for marriage… when there's plenty of love involved."

"She's so tiny."

"Well, only a few months, you know. Born last December."

"What's her name?" Violet asked innocently, approaching the baby. "Her tiny pink face, eyes shut tight, baby nose…"

"Her name is Rose," Jillian said, looking down at the little creature on her chest. "I call her Rose Bud."

## Chapter Twenty-Nine

# ROSE BUD

When Violet closed up the house on Basket Neck Lane after three more potential buyers had inspected it, she removed the sign from the driveway and placed it in the back of her car with the pile of brochures for the property.

She got into the driver's seat mechanically. All that had been echoing in her mind, the entire afternoon after Jillian had left, was the name, 'Rose Bud.'

She felt numb, almost sightless, so internalized were her thoughts, yet she managed to drive home to her house at the end of Shore Road, fortunately only minutes away.

Once inside, Violet sat on a corner of the sofa in the middle of the living room. It grew dark outside. Still, she sat, motionless, frozen inside with a sense of an ominous threat creeping into her life, as insidious as the ocean eating away at the grains of sand on Dune Road's beach.

Rose Bud. Rose Bud. The two words lapped at her mind like encroaching water.

"Violet, what are you doing, sitting there in the dark?

She was startled, as if wakened from a sleep. She had not heard the door open, nor the sound of his footsteps in the room.

Violet was silent a moment, then uttered the name, "Rose Bud."

"What?"

"Rose Bud."

Bud sank down next to her on the couch. "Violet..."

"Rose Bud?" Violet turned to him. She could only see his glistening eyes that caught the light of a rising moon.

"Who is Rose Bud?" he whispered.

"Jillian Burns' baby." At this, Violet rose to her feet. "Jillian Burns. Jillian Burns. She was the receptionist in your office, right? She was the one I had breakfast with – at her request – not mine – she, who at our wedding reception sat with Sasha."

Violet was pacing. "The two were so sour – oh I remember – even that happy day of days. They looked so mean," then, bursting from her, the question, "Oh Bud. Who is Rose Bud?"

"I swear I don't know." (He didn't.) He was on his feet beside her, reaching for her. "I don't know." His blood curdled inside him at the sound of the detested pet name Jillian had given him. It haunted him.

"Rose Bud is a baby!" Violet almost shouted at him. "Why would Jillian call her that? Why Bud? Were you and...?" but Violet could not continue the question.

"Please, honey...calm down. I have no idea why Jillian Burns would name her baby Rose Bud. Maybe she had a crush on me or something," he said feebly.

"A crush does not deliver a real live child, Bud! I saw her – the tiny little thing -" and she plopped back down on the couch.

"Where? How did this happen?"

"Jillian arrived at my Open House this afternoon. She had the baby swaddled around her chest. Oh, she was so smug, strutting around the place."

"Your Open House? My God, that was at an expensive property wasn't it? Why would she come there?"

"Because she knew I was inside. She saw my car parked out front. Bud, she came to SHOW me that baby. I know she did. Oh, God, she was so casual, so sure of herself!" and Violet burst into tears.

Now it was Bud's turn to pace. His mind in a turmoil, his hands shaking, he crossed and re-crossed the living room.

Finally, he sat down beside his wife, who was huddled on the couch, hands over her face, and tried to touch her. She recoiled. They were side by side saying nothing for several minutes. Only the sound of her hiccup-like sobs filled the room, slowly subsiding.

In a faint voice, at last, Violet said, "She's yours, Bud, isn't she! That baby. She's yours." It was not a question.

He said nothing.

"Isn't she?"

Slowly, a long guttural sigh from Bud filled the room. He could not speak.

Finally, Violet rose to her feet and headed toward the door to their bedroom. As she opened it, she turned to him and asked, "And just what are you going to do about it...her...Rose Bud? And what are you going to do about me?" She did not wait for an answer as she closed the door behind her.

At the mansion that afternoon, the baby had been silent in the folds of cloth at her mother's breast. In fitful sleep, this night, Violet dreamed a vivid dream, if you can call it that. It was only sound - the desperate wail of a child who is being swept away by crashing waves.

## Chapter Thirty

# THE MORNING AFTER

Bud had come home the previous night preoccupied with the car theft case. He could not wait to tell Violet of his suspicions in this department, only to find her so bereft and alone in the dark, with the name Rose Bud on her lips.

Rose Bud. A baby. Bud's earlier eagerness to be with his bride had turned into gall in his throat and a sickness of soul. He felt overwhelmed with what? Remorse? Guilt?

It could not be his! Bud slept on the couch.

Violet, in their large bed, in the bedroom with the door shut (not locked) had tossed and turned all night. How could Jillian have a tiny baby? Bud's baby, Violet was sure. The child, born in December, must have been conceived in March or April of last year. Violet counted the months. That was the very time Bud and she decided to marry, when he had asked her father for her hand, when they had decided to buy the house.

Bud must have been sleeping with Jillian Burns those same months.

Violet rolled over and buried her face in her pillow. It was at this moment, her husband tentatively opened the bedroom door.

He just stood there at the end of the bed. Finally, she roused up and sat upright against the headboard.

In a low voice, she said, "How could you have been with her – and with ME – at the same time? Did you make love to me one day and take her to bed the next? How did it work, Bud?" And then, in a pitifully small voice, she said, "I thought you loved me."

He was in tears. "I do love you Violet – with all my heart. Jillian – well, she was an outlet – so available, so fucking eager – and well, it was just there for me, I guess."

"'Fucking' eager is right! IT was just there for you? She was just there for you? What does that mean?" Violet was angry.

Bud perched on the end of the bed. "I have no excuse."

"How long was she 'there' for you? Months? Years?"

"A couple of years I guess."

Violet turned her face away. She could not look at her husband.

"Look, Violet – oh darling. Don't turn away. I never loved her…never promised her a future. It was just…well, for …fun, I guess. It was just… so available. I have no excuse, I repeat, but Jillian and I - we were never a couple. Christ, we never even went out in public."

"Well, I suppose you think that makes it all right."

"No, of course I don't think it all right – but I never led her on, let her believe we were having anything but a physical relationship…"

"A physical relationship? That's what you call it? Is that all WE have?"

"Of course not. I never loved her – never pretended I loved her – never mentioned the word love. And the minute you and I were truly engaged, I broke up with her. Believe me, she was not happy," Bud said ruefully.

"I'm sure. Her sexual nip-ups were over…IF they were over!" Violet said sardonically.

"Aw, Violet. I've had nothing to do with her since we got engaged. Look, I transferred out of the Sheriff's Office because of her, to be far away from her. I want nothing to do with Jillian Burns! Ever!"

"Why didn't you marry her?"

"Have you heard nothing I've said? I did not love Jillian Burns. I only love my one and only Violet Annas Rose. My Violet Rose." Bud took her hand, which was lying on the coverlet.

At this, Violet started to cry. Bud took her in his arms. Her tears wet his undershirt and his did too.

"Oh, Bud," Violet whispered. "There's a baby."

"I know. A baby."

"There's Rose Bud."

He got to his feet, rubbed his hand through his hair, his expression taut and troubled. "Christ. Rose Bud. It's may be another man's kid," he said, hopefully.

"Are you serious?" Violet reacted. "Just who, pray tell?"

"I don't know but there are other men in this town."

"Bud, you're reaching."

He sank down again on the bed. "I guess I am. Oh God. A baby."

Violet untangled herself from the sheets and walked across the room in her sleep shirt. Bud watched her. With her bare legs, and blonde hair tousled from sleep framing her face, he thought his heart would burst. He leapt up and embraced her, holding her close and murmuring into her hair how much he loved her. He could feel her trembling in his grasp and again the tears came for both of them.

"You have to see her," Violet said, her tone so low Bud could hardly hear. "You must."

"What would be the point?"

Violet looked up at him, startled. "It's your child, Bud, your own flesh and blood."

"What am supposed to do about that," he said, leaning back. "What can I say?"

"I haven't the least idea," and Violet walked out of the room.

# Chapter Thirty-One

# CONFRONTATION

The next morning, a hazy fog rested over Moriches Bay, as Bud started his car to drive to his office in Riverhead. The murky, humid atmosphere matched his deeply troubled thoughts. He was distraught over the discovery of Rose Bud and the cruelty with which Jillian Burns had inflicted that knowledge on his beloved Violet.

How in hell could he retrieve what he and Violet had created, the loving womb of the little house on Shore Road, the intimacy of their red-wine evenings, the warmth and laughter of his young bride. What must he do IF this child was truly his?

He made a detour. He hit Riverhead Road going out of Westhampton Beach, his siren going full blast as he turned into the Warehouse Storage facility at the Suffolk County Air Base.

The office was open. He sat in his car for a moment, bracing himself for what was to come.

Inside, Jillian Burns had set down her container of coffee from Seven-Eleven on the desk. She had taken off her kerchief from around her hair, when she heard the siren.

"It had to be," she said smugly to herself.

When Bud Rose had come into the office of the Storage Warehouse last week, Jillian was so shaken, she had decided to make a move, to begin the fight to regain his love. It might take bitter, lowdown, dirty methods of which she knew she was perfectly capable; hence, her visit with baby to Violet's Open House. When she had seen Bud Rose again, her desire for love – and revenge – was whetted beyond redemption.

"Vengeance is mine," she whispered to herself. "So is Bud Rose! and so is Rose Bud."

The door opened. He was there.

"Well," Jillian said after a long pause during which they stared at one another. "To what do I owe this visit? Or need I ask?"

"What in hell is going on, Jillian? I want the truth."

"Haven't you guessed?" She sat on her desk chair. "I thought you were bright enough, Bud, to figure it out." There was another pause. "You have a baby!"

Bud just stood there. "How do I know she's mine?"

"You can take a DNA test if you care to, but I can assure you, she's yours."

He had such a look of dismay on his face, Jillian continued. "What's the matter, Bud? Little Miss Violet not preggers yet? Something wrong with her plumbing?"

Bud stepped forward. He was ready to strike Jillian but refrained, his fists clenched. "You should be ashamed," he managed to say.

"Of what? And you, my dear, should be pleased with baby Rose Bud. Such a pretty little girl. I'm proud of her – and she's just as sweet as she looks." Then Jillian stood up, placing both hands on the desk. "I'm staking a claim, Bud Rose. This is your kid." Her voice was level, hard.

"What's that supposed to mean?"

"It means that I already have a lawyer. And guess who? He's the same guy who represents Bethany Brandeis – a Mister Mel Haddock. I call him Mr. Fish."

There was silence.

"You'll be hearing from Mr. Fish for the cash amounts in child support and of course, visitation rights. A little girl HAS to know her daddy, right Bud? And I'm sure little Miss Violet will make a grand step-mom."

Bud turned on his heel and slammed the door as he left, hard enough the glass in the top frame shuddered.

So did he.

Jillian at her desk did not.

# Chapter Thirty-Two
# 'THE HOTTEST ROD'

A week went by. Bud was relieved to go to work. The house was so mournful. He was still sleeping on the couch. He had yet to hear from "Mr. Fish" about baby obligations, but he knew that was to come.

So he was more than distracted by a call he received at his office on Howell Road in Riverhead. It was from a man in Greenport, a town out on the North Fork, who reported an accident.

"It's funny, officer. There's nobody in the car, but it's all the way over in the ditch...lots of skid marks. 'Course, it's been icy out here for the last week. But they just left the automobile here – like some dead animal."

"I sure appreciate your call," Bud responded into the receiver. "What kind of car?" His tentacles were up.

"It's expensive, no question, really spiffy," the man said wryly. "A bright silver color. New dealer plates."

Probably fake, Bud thought. "Do you know how long it's been there?"

"Well, it sure wasn't there yesterday. This is my route – come by here on my way to the restaurant this time every day, for my shift."

Bud thanked the man, got his name - Robert Grady -and the name of the restaurant – 'Orient By the Sea' at Orient Point, right next to the Cross Sound Ferry pier. "I'll be on my way," Bud told the fellow. "Wait there. I'd like to speak with you."

"No problem," was his answer. "What should I do about this car?"

"Are there people out there milling about?"

"No, sir. No one. Strange, you'd think it might draw a crowd."

"No police?"

"Uh uh."

"Well, you'd better call the Greenport police and tell them a detective from the Riverhead Special Unit Force is on his way and to leave the car. As is. You got that? The car should not be inspected, touched or towed, until I get there."

"I tell you what. I'll wait right here and protect it."

That's great, Mr. Grady. I'd appreciate it. You're a good citizen."

Before he left to go to the North Fork around 2:30 PM, Bud had called the Greenport Police and informed the detective on the phone of his conversation with Robert Grady. He reiterated the fact that he was from the Riverhead Special Unit Force, investigating a string of automobile thefts that had plagued Long Island the whole previous summer.

"This silver car could be one that was stolen, so please instruct any officers you send to the site that the car is not to be touched until I get there." Reassured, Bud got into his cruiser and drove as fast as the law allowed, and as he neared the crash, he turned on the siren full blast.

His first reaction was that the accident, although hard on the automobile, was probably non-life threatening to the driver, although certainly injury might have occurred. But, of course, no individual had been seen with the car, neither before nor after.

Bud climbed down toward the water, Robert Grady at his side. The driver's door was open, partially, and they managed to pry it wide. Bud, hands in plastic gloves, half-slid onto the seat. There was nothing of import to be seen at first, but then he found a stubbed out cigarette in the ashtray of the armrest. It had lipstick traces.

'Aha,' he thought, and bagged the stub.

Bud looked into the glove compartment. There were several papers that he took, and glancing through them quickly, he noticed one was a Storage Warehouse contract for unit number 103, one of the larger sheds at that facility. It was made out to "Magnates, Inc'.

"Now we're getting somewhere," he muttered.

"What?" Robert was standing outside, curious beyond measure. "By the way, the tow truck is here."

"Okay, okay," said Bud. "I want to see if we can open the trunk," he said to Robert as he got out of the car.

The tow truck driver had descended to join them at the site. He heard Bud's last remark and offered to get a metal hook from his truck. In minutes, the three men had pried open the trunk to find inside, a couple of tennis racquets and a dirty t-shirt in a ball in the corner.

Bud commandeered these items and turned the car over to the tow truck driver who was to take it back to police headquarters in Riverhead. The car was to rest in the police garage where inspection for fingerprints and other residue could be carried out.

"Thanks, Grady," Bud said, shaking the young man's hand. "You were a big help."

"My pleasure," was his response, with a grin. "I've never gotten involved in anything like this."

"Like what?" Bud asked.

"You know. A police investigation. A crime."

Bud gave him a smile and a pat on the back, went up to his cruiser and headed back to Riverhead. The first thing he did on regaining his office was to call Jordan Mather in New York and describe the situation – and the two tennis racquets and shirt.

"Sounds likely," was Mather's laconic response. Was this man so studied, so imperturbable Bud thought, or did he really not care? "Do you have any idea who took it?" Mather continued.

"Not yet, but we're getting close."

At the end of the conversation, as it was nearing 5:30 in the afternoon, Bud drove to the Storage Warehouse office on his way home.

It was closed.

"Tomorrow's another day, lady," Bud said aloud. "You and I have a date!" And he turned the nose of his cop car toward home.

# Chapter Thirty-three

## DITCHED

It was Jillian who had been driving the silver Corvette. It happened near 5:00 AM, just as she approached Orient Point. She had been through the town of Greenport, moving swiftly, surely, as usual. Driving the automobiles to the point of departure was one of her main duties for the group, who had given themselves the name: 'The Magnates'.

Jillian was paid well for each expedition, way above her Storage Warehouse salary and babysitting fees: $1000 per car!

She would drive to the Cross Sound Ferry pier, at the end of Orient Point, in order to be first in line to catch the 7:00 AM Cross Sound Ferry to New London. She would guide the car onto the ferry through its open rear maw on the lower level, making the vehicle the first one to drive off the ferry from the front, which opened out onto the gravel of the port in Connecticut. There, she would give the keys (and car) to a person the name of whom she never knew, a different man each delivery. He wore a small 'Magnates' button in the lapel of his coat.

Jillian would then always eat a large hot breakfast at the New London Diner, until time to board the noon Cross Island Ferry as passenger, returning to Orient point across Long Island Sound.

These winter days were cold on the ferry, but on arrival at Orient Point, she would walk, bundled up against the wind, to the Lobster Bar nearby, where Tad (Thadeusz) worked as a sous-chef. He would feed her a lobster roll, and she would wait there in the warmth and comradery of the small place until Sasha appeared. Sasha would drive her back to her flat in Eastport near King Kullen, often to spend the night in her bed. He still had no idea there was a Rose Bud in Jillian's life.

He would also, on these evenings, present her with $1000 in $100 dollar bills.

Jillian had been doing these 'transfers' all winter, starting out from the Storage facility near 3:00 in the morning, usually on a Saturday. It meant she would not see her baby that weekend, but the money was too good. This night in April was her sixth such trip. Each was different. Each car was luxurious, expensive, with the latest equipment, smelling of sweet, new leather.

It was a treat – a privilege- to drive the gorgeous machines. Jillian was thrilled with just being inside the handsome structures and able to handle the fine – and challenging – machinery. To be paid so well for doing so was the icing on the cake!

But icing of another kind – icing on the road – even in April - brought her sense of euphoria to a crashing end and a shrieking stop.

Jillian was in shock. Her head had hit the wheel and blackened her eye. The car had skidded off the side of the road toward water of an inlet and was smashed up against a tree that was now bent over almost in half.

The front end of the Corvette had a broken nose and, because of the impact, the hood had lifted exposing the engine's entrails.

She sat – half lay there - in the front seat for some minutes. She decided she was not basically hurt, except for the left eye, which she could feel swelling up. But what in God's name would she do about the car. She could not be seen in it or near it. It was a hot property.

Jillian untangled herself and managed to escape the Corvette. The door was hard to open but after several pushes with her legs, she managed to scramble out of the vehicle and up the small embankment to the road. She had the sense to take the car keys from the ignition. Adjusting her clothes, she then made her way to the Orient Point Cross Sound Ferry ticket office which opened at 6:00 AM.

A chilly dawn was beginning to light the edges of the landscape and the rim of Long Island Sound. It was an eerie glow, but soon enough, the little office opened its door, and Jillian was able to place a frantic call to Sasha.

"What!" was his immediate response. "How stupid! Where are you and where's the hell the Corvette?"

"In a ditch," she whispered into the phone.

"Jeez, Jillian. How'd this happen?"

"Ice," was her barely audible reply.

"In April?"

"It's still cold enough, particularly at this hour," she said crossly.

"Where are you now?"

She told him, and he shouted into the phone that he would leave right now to collect her and that she should not go near that automobile. "You get me? Don't go near it. You've never seen or heard of a silver Corvette, understand? Just stay put. I'm on my way."

Jillian nodded numbly, hung up and collapsed onto the nearest wooden bench. 'Ditched' she thought. 'I'm ditched.'

She waited for Sasha in the ticket office. As she sat there, still in shock, tapping her foot, Jillian decided she had to take off a day or two. She was shaken up from the unfortunate accident, nervous. 'I need something to distract me,' she thought uneasily. 'Anything to stop thinking about this.'

And then it came to her. While previously close to tears, Jillian now began to smile.

Her little weapon. Her Rose Bud. Ah yes, Jillian had a few more tricks up her sleeve.

## Chapter Thirty-Four

# THE WRONG CHILD

Violet was at her desk at Brandeis Realty. Her mouth, usually upturned in a smile, was a straight, if still voluptuous, line. Her shoulders were rounded, so different from the usual confident posture. And the lilt in her voice when she answered the phone was gone, replaced by a subdued and timorous tone.

"Everything all right *chez vous?*" was the cheery question from Bethany Brandeis who was observing her young employee with concern. "You don't look like yourself, Violet. Anything wrong?"

Violet shook her head, a little too vigorously. "No, no, Bethany. Nothing's the matter," and she tried to smile.

"Well, I can give you a piece of news that should make you grin from ear to ear." Bethany sat down in the chair next to Violet's desk. "Ed Conroy made an offer. It was a good one, not quite enough, but close enough for me to know he's serious and that we can make a deal. How's that for some happy news! It was your listing. You'll be getting your commission, Violet, and it's a big one. That should surely please that young husband of yours, no?"

"Oh, yes. Of course. That's wonderful. Bud…he'll be…"

"So proud of you," Bethany finished for her. "And he should be. You're a great asset, Violet. I want you to know that." Bethany sat there for a moment, studying the young woman. "I was wondering, dear, if you have thought at all about your father's house."

"What?" Violet was not expecting this. "Thought about his house?"

"Yes. You must realize that – not the house itself – but the property he's on – which is sizeable – and what a location! – It's enormously valuable. He could get a great deal of money if he chose to sell it."

"I'm sure he's never thought of selling it. He loves being where he is – and the stilts somehow protected us all from many a storm. I honestly don't think it has ever occurred to him to live anywhere else. After all, he's been there since the 50s."

"I know," Bethany said, "but there always comes a time – maybe for a change of life style – once one gets a little older. Anyway," she said, getting up, "why don't you ask him if he'd be interested. Hey, you never know… and think of your commission for that one." She patted Violet on the shoulder as she left and went back to her office.

Violet sat there a moment stunned. She felt Bethany had flattered her in order to use her in obtaining the listing for her father's house – her old home. For a moment, her depression disappeared, but soon returned in force. Rose Bud.

For the last weeks, since the knowledge of Rose Bud had entered their world, Bud and she had been distant and separate. He had finally returned to their bed, but she always had her back to him, and a simple, 'Goodnight, honey,' were his last words. He dared not approach her.

When they were first married – even on their honeymoon in New York City – the two had decided to wait to have a baby. They were having too much fun enjoying the discovery of each other in so many ways – especially, sexually. Their moments of desire were always a surprise and delight, sprinkled with intensity and lighthearted laughter, absolutely delicious.

But they were also discovering the nooks and crannies of personality that helped them really understand one another, where one could go and be accepted, and those narrow inlets that were dangerous to enter. The latter were few and far between for Bud. He was basically a straight and simple man – not stupid simple, but simple in nature. Violet was more complex, colored by her ambivalent love affair with the Atlantic Ocean. It pervaded her being.

The thought of bearing a child, for each of them, was put off for time to come.

"Maybe in a year or two," Violet would say.

"Or three," he might respond, pulling her to him. "In the meantime..."

But now, at her desk at the Brandeis Realty, Violet sat in hazy sorrow. There was a child, a child of Bud's, an unwanted one. What was he to do? How was she supposed to feel, and Jillian Burns – her arrogance at the Open House rankled in Violet's heart.

Poor little baby, Violet thought. Poor little child, and a teardrop fell on the schedule for house showings for the next day on her desk.

It was a slow day in the Real Estate office. Towards 5:00 o'clock, Violet collected her purse and a folder regarding a new potential listing she was to approach in the next days. She made her way to her car, parked on the side street behind O'Suzannah, a store featuring rather exotic imported Italian ceramics and tableware.

Violet was despondent on the drive back to Remsenburg. It was a soft evening, but her spirit was tortured with an inner grief. She knew Bud would not be home yet and her house would be empty.

As she turned into the driveway, she saw, propped up against the back door, a white sheaf. It contained flowers she could see, and suddenly her heart welled with love. Flowers! From Bud! She got out of the car quickly, clutching her purse and the folder, and ran to the back stoop.

Attached to the white paper holding the flowers, was a card. In large letters it said: 5 MONTHS OLD. Inside were five pink roses with tightly folded buds.

Violet burst into tears. All the pent-up sorrow seemed to explode inside her. She dropped her possessions – not the flowers – and ran around the side of the house and down to the small beach at the end of Shore Road. She was crying all the way.

There, on the sandy cove, she sat down, opened the paper and took the rose buds one by one and threw them into the bay. She tossed them as far as she could, the beautiful fragrant flowers that represented to her the height of betrayal.

"I'm drowning you, Rose Bud. You are gone forever. You don't exist," and she lay back against the sand, burying her head in her arms.

Bud found his wife there later that evening, lying inert on the little beach as the sun descended into Moriches Bay.

He picked up his wife in his arms and carried her back to the house. She murmured slightly, 'Rose Bud,' 'Rose Bud.' He laid her carefully on their bed, its white sheets clean and inviting.

Tears were in Bud's eyes, as he looked at Violet's sweet face, eyes shut, lashes long, casting a shadow on her cheeks. He caressed her face, her shoulder, gently. "Bud," she whispered. "Bud." It was a call.

"It's me Violet. It's always me for you," and he closed her tight in his arms and let the slow beating will of nature take control. "I love you, Violet."

"And I love you." They were together again. The pain was over, but not the agony of the unwanted child.

# Chapter Thirty-Five

# A BLACK EYE

For three days the Storage Warehouse office was closed. Bud checked the storage facility daily, not only convinced that Jillian was involved with 'Magnates, Inc.' but furious over her taunting Violet with the flowers. What a cruel, merciless act! Somehow, it had brought his Violet back to him, but what Jillian had done was unforgiveable.

Enough of the personal, he thought. Back to business.

He was positive now that the silver Corvette was indeed Rodney Mather's Christmas present. It was confirmed that the tennis racquets belonged to him, and there were his fingerprints on the gearshift.

There were fingerprints of another person as well on the steering wheel. Bud had these carefully secreted at the office.

It was a Wednesday that the office reopened. Bud was there mid-morning. He found Jillian, her back to him, checking a file cabinet. Over her shoulder she asked, "Can I help you?"

"I believe you can," said the policeman.

She turned slowly, on alert when she saw Bud in his officer's uniform standing before her. On his part, he was inspecting her face and upper body to see if there was any damage to her person, should she be the actual car driver.

And he found something: her left eye was blood shot and beneath the lower lid, on her cheekbone was an inordinate amount of tannish make-up. No matter how much she had applied, it could not disguise the yellowish/green bruise beneath her lower lid.

125

Bud said nothing.

"Well?" Jillian said. She sat at her desk.

"How'd you get the shiner?"

"None of your business."

"I think it is." With that, Bud pulled a paper from a small brief case. It was a copy of the contract for Storage Warehouse made out to 'Magnates, Inc.' "I was wondering, Jillian, just who this 'Magnates, Inc.' might be. You know, what kind of an outfit…"

"Where'd you get that?" Jillian said nervously, as Bud passed the paper to her. She glanced down at it, knowing full well what it was and who they were.

"Does it matter where I got it?"

"Of course," she said, sitting in her desk chair. "'Magnates, Inc.' is a customer. It's been with Storage Warehouse for a number of years."

"What's their business, do you know?"

She shook her head and busily rustled some envelopes on the desk in front of her. "I've no idea."

"Well, what do they store here?"

"How would I know? I'm just the receptionist/bookkeeper."

"And driver?" Bud said suggestively.

"Driver?" Jillian was trembling. She could not help herself.

"Yes, driver. Come on, Jillian. You're a nice girl and I know you wouldn't want to be involved with anything…well, not on the up and up," he said sarcastically. "Hey, can I sit down?" and he pulled up a chair and did just that. "Oh, by the way," he said with a big smile, "Thanks for the flowers."

Jillian blanched as she looked up at the face before her. She could not speak.

"You know, Jillian," Bud continued. "I think it best we close the office for now. I want you to come with me to police headquarters in Riverhead where I will have a few questions to ask you. In depth questions."

"What do you mean? I can't close the office. It's a busy business day for us – a week-day." She was really shaking now.

"Sorry, but I must insist. We'll take my car," he said pointedly as he rose from his seat. And they did, he supporting her left arm because Jillian looked ready to faint.

Rose Bud was not mentioned.

# Chapter Thirty-Six

# INTERROGATION

"If you cooperate and give me names, your situation could be greatly eased," Bud said to the woman sitting in front of him, quaking in her chair.

"What do you mean?"

"Ah, come on, Jillian, You know you're in trouble…crashing a car that was stolen – a very expensive vehicle…and I'll bet this was not the first time you drove a pricey automobile in the dead of night to Orient Point… to the ferry…because that was your destination, wasn't it?"

Jillian was mute.

Bud leaned back. He was in the swivel chair behind his desk in the Riverhead Police Department office. "Yeah. The good old Cross Sound Ferry to New London. Now, that would take you to a whole other State, right? A different jurisdiction." He leaned forward. "Let me see. 'Magnates, Inc.' Does that ring a bell with you? Just how much did they pay you?"

"I don't know what you 're talking about," she sniveled.

Bud stood up. "Well, I guess we'll just have to hold you as an accessory."

"On what grounds? You have no proof of anything."

"You're wrong, Jillian. We have your fingerprints on the steering wheel. We have the 'Magnates, Inc.' document, found in the glove compartment of the Corvette, defining exactly in which storage bin the car was housed… that was pretty careless of you to leave it there…"

"I was just the receptionist," she cried.

"Yes, and driver, and deliverer of stolen property. We even have a cigarette stub with lipstick on it which absolutely matches what you are wearing now."

"That could be anybody's."

"Look, I have plenty to hold you on. Now, stand up," and he pulled a pair of handcuffs from the top drawer of his desk. "Do you really want these?" he said, shaking the glittering cuffs before her.

Jillian burst into tears. "Bud. You wouldn't."

"Oh yes I would."

"What about our baby?"

"What?" He turned purple.

"Rose Bud. Our child," Jillian said, whimpering.

"You certainly haven't been much of a mother to her, now have you," Bud managed to say, voice rasping.

"She's with my Mom – in East Moriches. I see her as often as I can. I have to work, you know. A baby costs something to keep and care for…"

Bud was deeply bothered by the thrust of this conversation. "I expect to contribute to raising her – even though I've yet to hear from your lawyer – what'd you call him? Mr. Fish?" He paused, turned away, then, "That baby has nothing to do with the issue in front of us here and now."

"You call her 'that baby?'" Jillian was furious, crying. "How can I care for her if I'm locked away in a cage," she said, dabbing at her tears with a Kleenex.

"Listen," Bud said, sitting in a chair next to her. "You help me on this case in terms of giving me names of the perps, and I'll see that you are treated leniently…maybe a leg monitor…and you could stay up with your mother and take care of…Rose Bud." It was hard for him to mention the name. Then, he added pointedly, "No jail."

"You promise?" she whispered, flooded once again with a desire for him she detested in herself. She could not help the memories. He was so close, near enough to touch.

"I'll do my best…but we've got to get to the truth, Jillian. And I want it now."

"All I know is that there's this guy named Vinny in New York City, who seems to be the arranger – you know, to steal cars, stash them at the warehouse, then take them over to Connecticut to be sold. I think Tad, out at the Orient Point Restaurant, and Willie Yablonski did the actual robberies– hey, Willie works as a mechanic for your father-in-law at the Ford dealership on Montauk Highway," her last words said with a smirk. "Yeah, your precious father-in-law."

Bud was stunned. He said nothing. Then, "And Sasha?"

Jillian shook her head.

"Come on, Jillian. I know you two are having a go-round."

"What's that supposed to mean," she asked, sullen.

"You've traded me in for him."

"Says who?"

"It's common knowledge."

Jillian's head drooped. "He knows about all of it."

"He knows what about what?"

"About 'Magnates, Inc.' - about the car transfers to New London. But that's all," she said hurriedly.

Bud was satisfied. He had enough to pick up Tad and Willie. The NYPD would be contacted about Vinny – once the other two were in custody and talking, and as for Sasha? This was delicate for Bud. But Sasha would indeed be pursued, followed and subsequently interrogated.

Bud knew he was not a dispassionate interrogator – too much guilt, too much Rose Bud. However, Jillian's final words to him were the *coup de grace*.

She had looked up at him and said, in breathless tones, "Oh, Bud. Sasha and I – we're just friends. There's never been anyone but you."

He was startled.

"And I know," she continued, "you still care for me – it's still there, Bud..." and she reached up to touch his face.

"In your dreams, Jillian," Bud sputtered, grabbing her arm. "Now, let's get going!"

He arranged for Jillian's leg monitor and for a cop car to drive her to East Moriches, the prospect of which, Jillian met with dismay. How she hated motherly duties! Baby care did not become her - the diapers, the crying, the spit up. Her mother would be forced to continue what she had been doing all along. Jillian would sit before the television, leg monitor on her ankle, watching Reality shows and stewing in her own venom. This was to be her fate, she now realized, much to her disgust.

'I guess it's better than jail! she had to admit to herself.

Stella Burns was appalled when she looked out her window to the East Moriches Street and saw a cop cruiser pull up and daughter Jillian hobble out of the back seat on this late April afternoon!

A uniformed officer escorted her daughter to the door, knocked politely, and said, "Ma'am, Jillian here will remain at your home under house arrest. See that she stays put. You understand? She's to go nowhere," and he turned and walked away abruptly.

Jillian limped into the foyer, glaring at her mother. She could already hear the baby crying.

"What is this?'" Stella began, stunned by the whole incident.

"Don't. Don't, Mom. I'm in no mood." She walked into the living room.

"House arrest? What did you do? And why are you limping?"

"It's an ankle monitor so they know where I am at all times."

Stella sank onto the old sofa near the window. "Jill, just what is going on? I'm too old for this."

"I am too!" said Jillian sitting down beside her, raising her left leg and resting her foot on the ottoman. The ankle device was ugly and bulky. It was heavy too, and bit into her leg, causing bruising beneath the sock she wore.

The baby was crying even louder, and Stella rose wearily, left the room and returned, babe in arms. She tried to pass Rose Bud to Jillian who waved her away dismissively.

"What in hell is going on with you?" the older woman asked.

Jillian responded by contriving a story about a stolen car, that she didn't know was hot property, that it was all a big mistake, that her leg thing was only temporary.

"I would hope so," Stella said, but she did not believe her daughter for one minute.

Outside, the wind had picked up, and rain began to pelt the roof of the house.

"I have to make a call Mom."

"So make it."

"It's private."

"Of course it is," Stella said bitterly. She rose, carrying the baby and left the room, as Jillian went to the side table with its lamp and telephone.

Jillian's phone call was brief. It was, of course, to Sasha, with one word.

"Help!"

# Chapter Thirty-Seven

# A SLED?

"Rose Bud?" George Annas said, his face twisted with curiosity. He had been shocked when Bud had come to him and informed him of his illegitimate child.

It had been just two days ago that the young police detective arrived at George's office at the Ford dealership on Montauk.

"Ya have a minute, George?" Bud asked.

"For you, more than a minute," George said to his son-in-law, and he rose from his desk and closed the door behind Bud.

"A couple of things," Bud said.

"Hey, fella. You don't look so good."

"There's lots going on…lots on my mind," Bud replied. "First, you gotta guy working for you here named Willie Yablonski?"

"Well, I did. He quit a few days ago. Why?"

"Did he say where he was going?"

"No. Just that he was getting married and moving back to Polish Town in Riverhead and a new job. Didn't say much. It was pretty abrupt."

Bud sighed, his immediate source of information not available for the moment.

"Sorry I couldn't be of more help, Bud. Hey, what is it?"

"Can I sit down?" Bud looked pale.

"Of course. Here, here," George said, pulling up two chairs. And it was then that the story of Rose Bud and Jillian Burns and Violet's distress all burst from the tortured lips of Bud Rose. There were tears in his eyes when he spoke of his young wife.

Any thought of Sasha, George's son and his own brother-in-law, as a possible suspect in the car theft case, was lost to Bud, his emotion was so great over Violet's disappointment and sense of betrayal. Although he had planned to speak to George about Sasha, as delicately as possible – his movements, the levels of cash he displayed, his secretiveness – (Sasha still lived at home) – Bud was incapable of addressing any of this. He had started to cry over Violet, shamefaced and embarrassed.

George did not say much. He hadn't known how to respond, but he patted Bud's knee, said he understood how it could happen. His only question was 'Didn't you use birth control?' to which Bud had answered, 'Of course. But I guess it doesn't always work.'

"Rose Bud. Wasn't that mentioned in the movie 'Citizen Kane', you know, the movie we saw at the theater last winter" Anastasia asked.

"Oh yeah. I remember," George replied. "It was the trade name for the cheap little sled Kane was playing with when he was eight years old – the day he was taken away from his mom."

"I guess the sled was kind of a symbol of lost mother's love," Anastasia said, rising from the table and clearing away the dessert plates with the remains of whipped cream and chocolate cake. "Rose Bud," she muttered.

George sat back in his chair and lit a cigarette. "You're taking this all pretty calmly," he said to his wife.

Anastasia just shot him a glance.

"Rose Bud...and that woman Jillian Burns," George continued. He took a deep draft on his smoke, shook his head, and exploded in anger. "Why Bud would get involved..."

"Oh, come on George. Bud is a vigorous young man. He was single at the time. She was there in the office every day. Besides, there has been not one hint of him being with her since he and Violet married. He adores our daughter."

"I know. I know. But didn't they practice birth control – those two – Jillian and Bud? Damn stupid!"

"I think that woman got pregnant on purpose," Anastasia said firmly, as she sat back at the table.

"Would she really do that?"

Anastasia laughed. "Darling, you are naïve. It's the oldest trick in the world. I'm sure Jillian was dying to have Bud Rose all to herself."

"You mean marry him?"

"You bet. She's nobody's fool and Bud is a good man. She'd have been so lucky," Anastasia said wryly."

"Well, what do you know," George said. "You really think she tried to trap him?"

"But of course."

"Women!"

"Hey, I'm a woman," Anastasia said, grinning at him.

"Yeah, sweetheart. My kind of woman," and he leaned over and put an arm around his wife's shoulders.

Anastasia sighed and kissed him on the cheek. "Poor little baby. Rose Bud. What's going to happen to her?"

"I guess Bud's got to do something…child support at least. He told me that Jillian mentioned she'd already got a lawyer to go after him… the very lawyer who works for the realty company…a Mel Haddock."

"Why he was at Violet's wedding, remember? He came with Bethany Brandeis." Anastasia had moved off to the stove and was pouring two cups of coffee…black…the way they both liked it.

"Yeah," George said. "I remember. He wore a flower in his lapel… a sharp looking kind of guy."

"Well maybe he has to be. Most lawyers are."

"What?"

"Sharp," she said, handing him his cup.

"Boy, the wind is coming up," George said, suddenly. He could hear the front door creaking and rattling with the gusts.

"Guess so," Anastasia said. "Not another Nor-Easter! Enough already. It's not even May yet…too early for this."

"Well, you know…climate change and all that," George said, moving to turn on the radio next to the sofa in the living room. He listened briefly, came back to the kitchen and said, "Yep. It's due to be a big one. Better go down and check those stilts."

# Chapter Thirty-Eight

# ROSE

The storm was growing in intensity as Sasha arrived at the Burns house in East Moriches. He left his car, a Ford (of course) color gray, in the driveway and ran to the front door, drenched and panting.

Dripping wet, he entered the small front hall, apologizing for the puddle on the small rug. Jillian was there to greet him.

"God, it's rough out there," he exclaimed.

"Rough in here too," she responded quietly. "Come in." Stella Burns was behind her, carrying a terrycloth towel.

"Mom, this is Sasha," Jillian said, taking the towel and handing it to the man before her.

"Is he the baby's father?"

"No!" Jillian exclaimed, turning to her mother in anger. "Not Sasha. It's Bud Rose. Why do you think I named her Rose?"

"I have no idea," said Stella, "but to name a baby Rose Rose makes no sense," and she turned away, leaving the two alone.

"Baby?" Sasha exclaimed. He had dropped the towel.

"Rose Burns, Mom. Rose Burns," Jillian called after her mother with disgust. Then, "We're in trouble, Sasha."

"I gathered as much," he said in a nasty voice, picking up the towel and busily drying himself, his coat, his hair, even his shoes. "What's this about a baby?"

"I'll explain all that later. Come in," and she led him into the living room.

139

"What'd you tell the police?" he questioned.

"As little as possible," Jillian said. They were speaking in hushed tones. Stella was nowhere about, but still, the two culprits had good reason to be fearful and cautious.

"I've got an ankle monitor. Clumsy thing. My whereabouts can be checked by the police in Riverhead, no matter where I go."

"Yeah," he said. "Radio frequency signal, back to their monitoring station."

"I have to charge the battery every 12 hours. Pain in the ass. And besides, the damn thing hurts."

"Look, I can cut the fiberoptic cable, but that means the police will get an alarm."

Sasha was dry enough for the two to sit on the sofa. "Listen," he said. "We've got to get out of here. We've got to go on the run, Jillian."

"Oh my God."

"What else? Do you want to spend time in prison? I sure as hell don't!" Sasha was now up and pacing. "I was smart enough – when I heard about all this – to clear out my bank account. I have a load of cash with me. Do you have any?"

"Not much," Jillian said. "I didn't have a chance…"

"It's okay for the moment. The important thing is to decide where to go, where we can hole up until this thing hopefully blows over. We have to disappear – and that means no baby. Who…what is this baby thing?" he sputtered.

"You remember when I kind of disappeared for a few months last fall?"

"Yeah. Huh! 'Kind of disappeared'," he said with sarcasm. "And without a word."

"Well, I came here…and well, I guess…Rose Bud is the result."

"Rose Bud?"

"It's Bud's kid."

"Good God! Not my brother-in-law's?"

Jillian nodded.

Sasha burst out laughing, mostly from nerves. "So, it's all in the family! I can't believe it." He sat down again. "You'll have to leave her here. There's no way we can take her with us, you got that Jillian?"

"No baby," she said softly.

"Your Mom can take care of her. She's apparently already doing it anyway," he said in snarky fashion.

Jillian glared at him. "Okay. I get it. But just where are we to go? Maybe we should just ditch the car in the water and…disappear for real?"

"Kill ourselves?" he said with a grin.

"Just an idea," she said glumly.

"It's a thought," Sasha said, sitting back on the sofa beside her. "The storm is sure strong enough to have an accident. In any case, we have to determine where we want to end up. You might have to dye your hair – and I grow a beard – but all that's do-able."

"How about the Big Apple?"

"Nah," he said. "Neither of us know it well enough – better out here – say, Hampton Bays – somewhere on the South Fork – the police may assume we might go to Orient again and cross over to Connecticut. Let's hope they do. But we can really stay near the ocean."

"How about this?" Jillian said. "Let's drive by way of Dune Road to Hampton Bays. There are lots of little out of the way places in the area. We can tell Mom we're going to Orient Point. She'll believe it and tell the police who will surely come here once my ankle device is shut down. The minute the cable is cut, it will send an alarm."

"Yeah! We stay on the South Fork and the cops are sent to the North Fork. Good thinking! Now, you have any tools?"

"In the garage…but we have to do this right now?"

"Jillian, time is of the essence. We have to move quickly. Better start packing something – as little as possible - and begin saying your goodbyes. Now, how do I get to the garage?"

"Outside…you'll get wet again…" Sasha just glanced at her and went out the front door, as Jillian put her head in her hands. There was even a tear or two…but not many.

Bud got the call near 8:00 PM from The RPD that Jillian's monitor signal had ceased. He was at home on Shore Road, busily battening down the windows and doors, thanking his lucky stars for having the new stanchions, because the storm was beginning to come in hard and heavy.

He was alarmed. He knew that Jillian had been at her Mom's with Rose Bud. He determined he had to drive there to make sure the child was safe. Mrs. Burns' house was inland which was a good thing under the circumstances, even safer than his own home.

He called to Violet who was more than willing to leave Shore Road as the bay mounted threateningly toward them, and the reeds grew soaking and mushy. The two took her red coupe and headed toward East Moriches.

As Bud drove through storm, Violet seemed to hear a baby crying. She knew it wasn't real, but the sound of the high wind and violent rain could not drown out the whimpering child. They arrived at Stella Burns' house, only to find that Sasha and Jillian had gone.

"Went up on the North Fork," Stella Burns declared. "Headed toward Orient…don't know why."

Bud realized they had probably passed them on the road – the red coupe and the gray Ford, going fast in the rain, an ultimate irony.

Stella Burns was alone with the baby. Bud and Violet decided to hunker down there in Mrs. Burns' house for the night. It was safer than the roads, safer than their own place on Shore Road.

For the first time, Violet took Rose Bud in her arms. The baby looked up at her and stopped crying.

That same night, Sasha was driving Dune Road as it swerved up toward Hampton Bays, a tricky turn, particularly with the pounding wind, streaking rain, and ocean water spilling over the dunes and onto the road itself. Jillian was huddled and fearful next to him.

The gray Ford was suddenly overcome by a huge wave that pulled it into the deep. Sasha gunned the motor, which sputtered. They were going fast as Jillian yelled, her final words, "Christ, Sasha. Are you really trying to kill us?" as the car turned over and rolled in the surf.

Two days later, when the storm had eased away, the sky was cloudy, and workman began to clear the toppled trees. Electricians were on ladders adjusting downed power lines. It was only then that the side of the Ford edged above the calm ocean water line. It was difficult to see because the gray car was the color of the waves.

It was spotted from the shore by two adventurous souls who were out on the beach, looking for odd things washed up during the tempest now passed, odd items like a kitchen pot, an empty picture frame, warped by water, a child's soggy teddy bear.

"What in hell is this?" the young man exclaimed. And there, lying in the sand was a device, half cut in two with a belt attachment.

"Yeah, what is it?" said the girl, picking it up.

"Hm. Looks to me like some sort of ankle bracelet. It's too big for a wrist – too small for a leg …but an ankle…?"

Then suddenly they saw the car, water lapping against it gently.

"Good God," the young man shouted.

"Oh, Lord," said the girl. "We'd best get the police!" and the two ran up to the nearest dune house where they saw people moving to make the call.

No bodies were ever found.

"Taken out to sea, no doubt," the policeman said. "Those waves were immense."

"And they probably ended up food for the fishes," the young man piped up.

The policeman gave him a look. It was one of the biggest storms ever to hit the East End, causing damage all the way to Montauk. Even some of the shingles from the famed lighthouse at Montauk's tip had been ripped away.

George Annas' house in Westhampton Beach lost one of its stilt legs for the first time ever, the building crazily atilt on the sand dune. No one was hurt. Of course, the house was put to rights within hours, by George, and a new stilt leg installed and buttressed, deep into the ground.

"To live to see another storm," he said to himself, happy in the thought his little world would survive them all.

The Weather Service gives title to all such tempests during the year. And for this one, what else?

The name of the storm was ROSE.

# "THE ROSE" Trilogy

**Violet Rose,** is the first book in a trilogy where the ocean is metaphor for the turbulence in the lives of Violet, her husband, Bud Rose, their enemies and friends. The setting is the East End of Long Island, New York, where love, money, and drama are principals. Yet, here too, the sea evokes beauty and respect for its limitless power. In Herman Melville's Moby-Dick, the ocean is presented as "mystic... that deep, blue bottomless soul."

**Starfish,** book two, continues life on Long Island with Bud and Violet. A mysterious crime occurs as the hurricanes and tempests beset them, and a small girl, a part of their lives, encounters danger from out of the past.

**Violet,** the third book brings the ocean waters deep into Long Island. The storms increase over time, in depth and intensity (due in large part to climate change), mirroring the violence and malevolence of the characters. Ultimately, the whole island is threatened, as is the city of New York. Bud, Violet, and their loved ones are directly in the path of the encroaching sea as it sweeps across their world.

CPSIA information can be obtained
at www.ICGtesting.com
Printed in the USA
LVOW11s0237120517
534206LV00001B/1/P

9 781458 221018